MW01452486

# Nothing Left to Give

## Lori Bell

This book is a work of fiction. Names, characters, places, and incidents are the product of the author's imagination or are used fictitiously. Any resemblance to actual events, locales, or persons, living or dead, is coincidental.

Copyright © 2022 by Lori Bell

All rights reserved. This book or any portion thereof may not be reproduced or used in any manner whatsoever without the express written permission of the publisher except for the use of brief quotations in a book review.

Cover photograph by CanStock Photo

Printed by Kindle Direct Publishing

ISBN 9798427567893

# DEDICATION

It's not what happens to you… it's how you react to it.

# Chapter 1

Jacobi. That's who she was known as. At Cleveland Clinic, however, the honorific title of *doctor* preceded her birth-given last name. At 35 years old, Reese Jacobi had been practicing obstetrics for seven years following more than a decade of medical school, clinicals, and residency.

Three babies were born in the wee hours the previous night, which meant Jacobi's shift at the hospital was now going on 24 hours. She held a steaming coffee mug in one hand and coincidentally its dark blue hue matched her navy scrubs. She shuffled her feet — relishing the comfort of the soft, lightweight, white, slip-on loafer with elastic laces that never failed her on those hospital floors for hours on end. She was enroute to the nurse's station for an update on her just-admitted 29-year-old patient, who was on the cusp of becoming a first-time mother to twins. She took another step when a door to her left swung open and Ben Oliver invaded her path. Her coffee swirled too close to the top of the mug in her hand as she shifted her body to prevent a collision with him. She saved herself from colliding and spilling, respectively.

"I heard you were called in," Jacobi noted. Delivering babies had kept her moving steady all night, but just before sunrise she knew he was in the building. His voice carried on that OB floor. Women highly respected him as their doctor. He was damn good, and equally as good looking.

He nodded. "This one is stubborn. It's only a matter of time before we prep for a C-section."

"By stubborn you're referring to baby or momma?"

He grinned with a subtle eye roll, while Jacobi stifled her laughter and the two of them veered off path and stopped at their same nurse's station destination. Ben Oliver had been an obstetrician ten months longer than Jacobi. They met in medical school, and both ended up doing their residency at Cleveland Clinic. Their paths continued to merge, as they were now practicing at the same hospital. Their friendship was as solid as their working relationship. Completely trusting each other as professionals stemmed from bonding as friends first. From every angle, the two of them were an integral part of each other's lives. Ben was married to a woman that Jacobi had come to claim as one of her closest friends. The women, Marti and Jacobi, were complete opposites. Marti was blonde; Jacobi was brunette. Marti was petite and generously curvy at 5'3", while Jacobi was leggy at 5'7" and toned in all the right places. Marti was a business major in college but had never contentedly settled into one specific career; Jacobi was as career-driven as they come, solely focused on being a doctor. That was her passion; her whole life.

Ben and Marti were married five years, and they shared a two-year-old little girl named, Suzie. Jacobi had an honorable role as their child's auntie, which she cherished with every ounce of her being. Adorable little Suzie genetically inherited a full head of blonde spiral curls from her mother, and those big brown eyes were just like her daddy's.

After they congregated at the nurse's station, Ben made his way to the locker room. It was a unisex space that was partitioned for privacy. As the door to it was closing on its own, Jacobi passed by.

Ben called out to her, as she took a step back, caught the door with her free hand, and entered. They were the only two people in there, but the room typically had a revolving door from the medical staff coming and going around the clock. The thought crossed Jacobi's mind that he was already wearing scrubs and not in there for a quick change of clothes. Not that Jacobi had never seen him shirtless before, or more. That memory had a way of resurfacing.

The door closed behind her and she took a generous sip from her coffee. "I want to run something by you," she heard him say. She made eye contact with him but never spoke. The two of them felt at ease with shared silence of any kind. They knew when to stop and listen. They often asked each other for professional advice, and their personal lives were so interconnected that no topic was ever off limits. Even still, Jacobi wasn't sure if she heard him right this time.

"What did you say?"

"Marti wants to try again, but I think it's too much for her to handle emotionally."

His words, *try again*, meant for another baby. Jacobi sighed at Ben's admission, partly because she agreed with him. Two miscarriages in the last year would take its toll on any woman. Apparently conceiving Suzie happened easily but, as specialized doctors, both Jacobi and Ben had tried to explain to Marti that second child infertility was indeed a thing.

"So, you've told her that you're not ready to put yourselves through that again?"

"I explained that we shouldn't push for this or rush it. That's the thing. It will happen when it happens, but she wants Suzie to have a sibling close in age, and Marti claims that being in her mid-thirties is also a reason for the urgency to get pregnant now, have our second child, and be done."

Jacobi felt that mid-thirties truth more than anyone knew. She delivered hundreds of babies a year and handed them over to their mothers. Yet she had never been a mother herself. She wished to personally experience pregnancy and childbirth; it just didn't seem to be in the cards for her. "Do you want another child with Marti?" She looked him in the eye as he stood in front of his open locker.

He seemed to take a moment to ponder her question or overthink his answer. Finally, he said, "I love my little girl more than anything... and I know that if we cannot have another baby, she's enough for me."

"Have you told Marti that?"

"God, no. She's not ready to hear that or especially to believe it herself. She's so consumed with the idea of having another. Sex between us has become solely about the act of conceiving." Jacobi looked down at the remaining coffee in her cup. She didn't need for him to put that image in her head. It was more than enough at times when Marti shared the intimate details of their bedroom…or the shower…or against the door of the playroom during naptime. "Sorry," Ben noticed the awkwardness in her body language. "I just can't, and I don't know how to tell Marti that. I guess I needed to tell someone."

"And I'm that lucky someone," Jacobi winked, having completely recovered from the weird vibe between them just seconds ago.

"You know us well, and all we've been through," he defended. "Maybe you could talk to her?"

"Me? What am I supposed to tell her? A woman wants what she wants…"

Ben laughed out loud, as the door swung open and one of the nurses stuck her head inside. "Dr. Jacobi, we're fully dilated and ready to begin pushing."

"And that's my cue to go," Jacobi spun on her heels and caught the door from the nurse who had already darted off, down the hallway.

"Saved by the birth!" Ben called after her.

She giggled. "Right."

"Wait. Just throw out something for me, STAT. You always give the best advice."

Jacobi poked only her head through the doorway. She was very good at reacting under pressure. She said what came to the forefront of her mind. "Try to give your wife what she wants."

She was in the hallway when the door had not fully closed again and she heard him say, "I don't know if I can."

Dr. Jacobi had a patient in labor waiting on her, as well as a team of delivery staff expecting her expertise and flawless guidance. She forced herself to put that first. It's what she did. It was her means of survival; a method to mask the heartache. She let the door to the locker room close, turned her back, and reluctantly walked away.

# Chapter 2

Twin girls were born just two minutes and thirteen seconds apart. They were fraternal twins, as their conception had been successful through the help of in vitro fertilization. Two strong eggs defeated the odds, and Jacobi blinked back the tears in her own eyes as she handed the 29-year-old mother her babies, one for the crook of each arm.

"Thank you for everything you've done to make this happen, Dr. Jacobi," the woman's words were filled with genuine gratitude. She held her two precious gifts in her arms, and credited Jacobi for making that dream become a reality. An emotional father of the babies echoed those sentiments, as Jacobi gracefully accepted their appreciation and then congratulated the first-time parents before she left the delivery room. She was still smiling to herself when she stepped into the hallway with a veteran OB nurse on her heels.

"You do good work, honey." Reeda was a fifty-something, hefty, black woman who mothered everyone under that hospital roof, patients and doctors alike.

Jacobi smiled. "This feeling never gets old, that's for sure. I am able to be a part of something where there's so much love and hope felt for a tiny human who has entered the world for the very first time."

"Ah yes, so well said," Reeda gave her a side hug before they walked in opposite directions.

The childbirth high had worn off as Jacobi sat down on the sofa against the wall in the locker room. She bent forward, put her face in her hands, and closed her eyes for a moment. Sleep was summoning her. Being on call for those multiple births last night meant she had not been able to go home, and now she would end up working a 36-hour shift once today was done. She needed more coffee or something substantial to eat. Her thoughts were interrupted when the door to the locker room swung open. The surgical cesarean section was complete. After any surgery, Jacobi noted that Ben was typically sweaty. The hair around his ears was matted and curling, and the neckline of his scrubs was damp. If he lifted his arms, Jacobi was certain she'd see pit stains.

He saw her on the sofa, but she was the one who spoke first.

"How'd it go?"

"Uneventful. Still a miracle." It's what he told his patients, especially those women who had concerns about not being able to naturally give birth. *Would the experience be any less heartfelt?* Dr. Ben Oliver always reassured them of the wonder of childbirth simply being a miracle any which way it happened.

"Good," she reacted, trying to will herself to stand up and get her body moving again. She could have taken a quick catnap in there, but Ben's interruption was okay with her.

"Are you seeing patients today?"

She nodded, sleepily.

"How many hours are left for you here?"

"Sevenish," she answered.

"You're beat."

"So what?" she sassed him.

He laughed. It was so easy with her. The beautiful, career-focused, twenty-something young woman that he met in medical school had become a lifeline for him. A confidant like no other — not even his wife.

He sat down beside her.

"Can we continue what we were discussing earlier when you walked out on me?" he purposely teased her to rile her.

"Childbirth comes first, asshole."

He stifled a chuckle and nudged her bicep with his elbow. Jacobi ignored the sensation she felt from that.

"I don't want to repeat the lows of the last year. I can't watch my wife lose another baby that we want too much. I mean that. Did you ever want something too much? Nothing good comes from that."

His words were true. Truer than he realized, she assumed. The bond between Jacobi and Ben was airtight, and primarily existed as strictly platonic. Neither of them had ever wanted to cross that line. They both loved Marti and all that she brought into their lives. There was never obvious desire, or temptation. Neither would risk ruining their solid friendship, or intentionally hurt Marti.

Soon after Ben and Marti met, she pushed him for a commitment, all while he opposed rushing their relationship. He was clear about wanting to date her and only her, but she adamantly pressed him for a marriage proposal. She handpicked her own engagement ring and then sent him to the jeweler. *"The hard part is done... all you have to do is buy the ring and choose the time and place to ask me to marry you... and you know I'll say yes."* Jacobi and Ben have repeatedly shaken their heads and laughed about Marti's less than subtle ways. She could be demanding, but that was just Marti. She didn't know how to let up until she got what she wanted, or thought she needed.

On the night before their wedding — after the rehearsal at the church, dinner afterward, and many celebratory drinks — the wedding party dispersed. Marti forced each of them to promise not to arrive late to the church the following day. She was the first one to leave the gathering, as she'd sworn she needed seven hours of beauty sleep. That left Jacobi to give Ben a ride back home. She assured Marti that she would get him home safely and timely. He had an apartment then, near the Cleveland Metro Parks. It was just a short drive from the nightlife of the Kamms Corner Area, where they had been celebrating.

Jacobi walked Ben inside his apartment that night, which was not out of the norm as she shared a mutual admiration for his dog. The same dog that Marti had never warmed to, and they had still been arguing about Ben moving into her townhouse with his dog once they were married. Marti did not want to have a pet, but Ben hadn't backed down, and he and Jacobi were discussing the ridiculousness of that issue at his apartment that night. He poured her a glass of wine while she doted on his dog.

She already had three margaritas at the Mexican restaurant. "One glass, and I have to go. I can't be hungover tomorrow!" Jacobi halfheartedly teased him.

"Or late!" Ben had wagged a finger at her, mocking his fiancé's anal ways, and then he tipped back a drink of wine straight from the bottle.

"You stop. She means well. That's just our Marti being Marti."

"Our Marti," Ben repeated her words then. "Like we share her or something."

"What does that mean? She's become one of my closest friends. I love her, too."

"I know that. I just wonder what our lives would be like if…"

"Don't." Jacobi had suddenly felt sober.

"You don't even know what I am going to say." Jacobi kept silent and stared at him. She was suddenly finished with giving her attention to his dog. Ben stood near the kitchen counter and she was an arm's length away from him. "She's a straight-arrow, and I don't always love that about her. I mean, she's never done anything wrong. She hasn't the slightest clue what it feels like to just let go. Just do. Just be. And then worry about the consequences later, if you even have to."

"You're only saying these things because you're scared. It's the night before your wedding. You've got cold feet."

Ben ignored the excuses she made. "You're not like her."

Jacobi shrugged and reached for her glass of wine from the countertop, as she needed another sip. This conversation was getting uncomfortable between them. They had never addressed this before. What was, or could be, between them had always been off limits. Unspoken.

"You're right. I am not like her," she finally answered him. "I prefer to freely test the waters myself instead of joining everyone else wearing their life jackets as they jump in feet first."

"You like the deep end," he already discovered that about her.

"Absolutely. I dive right in. You won't find me inching my way into the shallow end. I like the shock of the water on my skin before my brain even realizes what's happening."

"I've drifted from living like that," Ben admitted, regretfully, and he drank more wine.

"We all have to grow up some time," she halfheartedly teased him, but she believed in her soul that she would never be like everyone else, not for the wrong reasons.

"It's not about immaturity and you know it," he called her out.

"Stop reading me so well," she nearly whined.

"I can't. It's who we are. And how we are together. We make a damn good team, Reese."

"It's Dr. Jacobi to you," she belted out a silly, drunk laugh.

"Nahh… it's Reese."

"That's weird to me. It doesn't even feel like my name. I'm Jacobi. Always have been."

"That's because you want to appear tough. Call me by my last name. It's catchy. It's high-powered. But I see you. Reese. The woman behind it all."

She blushed. She was never embarrassed, especially not around him. She reached for her wine glass on the counter again, but this time she missed taking hold of it. She bumped the side of the glass and it toppled over. When it fell on its side, wine spilled down the cabinet door and onto the floor.

"Shit. She reacted, and lunged for it, but Ben intercepted. He stopped her. He touched her. *Was the world still turning?* Together, they looked at each other. *Differently?* Not really. The connection between them was always evident and strong, but they both had fought it for far too long. They had to. For their jobs. For Marti.

"Please leave it," he barely spoke those words, and his hand was still on her forearm. "Sometimes we just have to make a mess and leave the cleanup… or the repercussions… for later."

"Live in the moment. That's what you're saying, right?" she asked him, and for the first time in what felt like forever, she didn't care about anything. Neither of them were thinking of honoring Marti because they loved her and respected her feelings. This was only about them.

He nodded. "A carefree moment."

"Just for tonight," she suggested as if she was searching for that reassurance from him. "Then, tomorrow, it's business as usual."

"It's my wedding day, not a workday," he chuckled.

"You know what I mean."

"I always know what you mean," he touched her face with his open palm, and they closed the space between them.

~

Ben nudged her again on the sofa in the hospital locker room. "Do you agree with me or no?"

"Yes, it can be unhealthy to want something too much," she responded, "but that's not to say that you shouldn't try very hard to get it."

"I'm just done with the pain. I don't see why we can't just live our lives and not force a pregnancy to happen."

"You're contradicting yourself as an obstetrician," she called him out. "I just helped deliver twins who would not exist if we hadn't made it happen in the lab. That's forcing pregnancy to work to give people what they want. Why is that so different for you as a man than as a doctor?"

"I don't know," Ben admitted. "It just is."

"I think you do know," Jacobi pressured him. "What are you not admitting here? Marti is young and healthy. She's already had one successful full-term pregnancy, so it isn't impossible for her to have another. It's proven to be more difficult after two miscarriages, yes, but again, not impossible."

"I don't want another baby."

Jacobi turned to the side and stared at his profile. There was some scruff on his face which was rarely ever there. He was called in for an emergency before he had the chance to give his face a clean shave first thing this morning. She remembered seeing the scruff on his face years back, the morning after. She had never forgotten how it felt against her skin either.

She forced herself to focus on what he had just said.

"Why? You're a wonderful father. Suzie is so in love with her daddy. The job you're doing with raising her, you and Marti both, has taught me so much. I mean… if I ever have the chance to be a mother… I would adore my child exactly the way you two do."

"I don't want another baby," he repeated, "with my wife." Jacobi's eyes widened. She was stunned speechless. "I love her, but not in the heart-pounding, breathless way that a man is supposed to love a woman. I can't see forever with her anymore. I want to, but I can't."

"Oh my God, Ben," Jacobi finally spoke. "You have to work hard and fight like you've never fought before to save your marriage. Rekindle the damn flame!"

"You're not hearing me. The flame never sparked an inferno. Not like—" he turned to look at her. She stood up abruptly. So suddenly that she felt unsteady on her feet. She needed to find her sense of balance quickly.

"Stop. We promised we wouldn't revisit that again." She took a few more steps away from him, closer to the door.

"Do you ever think about it, though? I mean, in secret, in the privacy of your own memory?"

"What I remember," she avoided his direct question, and purposely remained distanced from him in that locker room, "is the morning after. It was your wedding day. I told you that I loved you, and you professed those same words back to me."

"But I married her anyway," he interjected, retelling the story as if she had not known how it all panned out.

"We had our chance," she spoke as a matter of fact. "Or, we had our one night of intense passion. Whichever way you choose to perceive it."

"How do you see it?" Ben asked her outright.

"You said it best just now… about wanting something too much. Nothing good comes from that."

There was no way around the pain of regret, and Ben had not felt the worst of it more deeply than now. "Did you really want me to leave Marti at the altar that day?"

"I really wanted it to be you," she confessed the words that she never dared to say to him before. "I so badly wanted it to be you. Until I understood, watching you marry her that day, that you didn't want it to be me."

With that said, Jacobi turned her back and walked out of the locker room just as another hospital staff member entered.

She was halfway down the hallway before she was able to catch her breath. That was a hard truth, one that Jacobi had never spoken to him or to anyone. It had been painful enough just to admit it to herself.

# Chapter 3

Avoidance. It was the only way that Jacobi was going to get through her overtly honest exchange with Ben earlier. Yes, they worked together. Same hospital. Same floor. But most times there were too many other people around them to have a private conversation. She would also make a point not to be alone with him in the locker room. At least not for a while. An exchange between them like this morning could not happen again. Jacobi was adamant about that. He had a wife and a child. Ben needed to put his marriage and his family first. And Jacobi needed to continue to keep her feelings at bay for the only man she knew she would ever love. If she couldn't have him, she didn't want to know that feeling with anyone else. It's the way she lived her life. She was hardly celibate, as she went on occasional dates with other men, and she had sex. But that's all it was. A physical need being met; she kept her heart out of it.

At the end of her shift, Jacobi saw her last patient for what she hoped would be until tomorrow morning. The only thing she wanted to do was go home and fall into bed, but all it would take was someone's water to break during the night to call her back there. It was her way of life. Her trade. The career that she worked tirelessly for and could not love more.

She closed her locker door and turned away from it with her purse already on her shoulder. She looked before she took a step; she didn't know anyone else was in there until she turned and saw him. He straddled the bench near her locker.

"So, what? You're avoiding me now."

"I've seen you all day long. I work here."

"You know what I mean."

"All I want to do is go home and sleep."

"I know," he sympathized, and he understood. Even overtired, she was on top of her game in that hospital. And, Ben had tried not to ever notice, but she looked adorable with sleepy eyes. He chided himself every time he relived their night together in his memory, but he did it anyway. He remembered how they never gave into much sleep. Their desire, the reality that they were finally together in the most intimate way, had given them both a lasting adrenaline rush. Making love once had not been enough for either of them. And when they let each other go in the morning, what happened between them stayed only between them.

Jacobi looked at him. She stepped closer and kept her voice low. "Ben don't do this. You are my best friend, my colleague. I adore your wife and little girl. I can't even express to you how badly I want things to stay as they are." She started to move past him, and once again it was her intention to walk away.

"Stop running," he stood up to block her way.

She stared at him. She was utterly exhausted, physically and now emotionally. "Think of Marti."

"This isn't about her."

"The hell it's not!"

"You know what I mean."

"Stop saying those words to me. What I know is how to move past what happened, and up until today I believed that's what we both had done."

"Have you really?"

"Yes!"

"Then why aren't you with someone?"

"I don't have to be with anyone to be fulfilled in my life." She closed her eyes and sighed heavily.

He gave in. "Go home. Get some rest."

He stepped aside then, and she walked past him, but before she reached the door he spoke again.

"Jacobi…"

"What?"

"I don't believe you."

~

Despite how Ben Oliver stirred her emotions, Jacobi went home, stripped off her scrubs, and indulged in a hot shower before she fell into bed and slept twelve solid hours. She woke up to her alarm at 5 a.m.

She laid back in her bed with her cell phone in her hands once she turned off the alarm on it. It was then that she noticed two missed text messages. Both were from Marti, and the time sent on those messages was yesterday while she was still at the hospital finishing her shift. She had not taken a moment to check her phone after work. She was too tired. And she was also spent from the emotionally charged exchanges with Ben.

The messages from Marti were typical, yet Jacobi found herself reading into them more than she would have otherwise.

*Call me when you have time.*

*I really could use your insight on something important.*

Jacobi knew that Suzie was an early riser, so she didn't second guess texting Marti back.

*Sorry I'm just now seeing your texts. Worked a 36-hour shift and crashed last night. I'll call soon. Promise.*

Only a few minutes passed before Marti sent a reply. Jacobi was just about to step into the shower when she reached for her phone again.

*I get it. I'm married to your work buddy. Talk soon, Cobi.*

The first half of Marti's text guilted her. Ben had been so much more than her buddy. How she signed off, though, made her smile. Adorable little Suzie's way of saying her name always made her day.

~

When Jacobi had a patient cancellation right before her lunch break, she took her cell phone outside and called Marti.

"Hey, is this a good time?" Marti was currently in-between jobs and had not cared about working. She did that sometimes, especially since Suzie was born, but that was alright as Ben's salary could support them during those lulls.

"It is a good time. Sooz is actually napping."

"I'm on break, so I thought I'd check in to see what's on your mind."

"It's Ben," was all she said. Jacobi closed her eyes and inhaled the fresh air outside and listened. She feared that Marti's worry had everything to do with trying to get pregnant and sensing that her husband wasn't all-in anymore. And she was right. "He's not as ready as I am, to try again for another baby."

"Is that what he told you?" Jacobi was careful to form the right words.

"Not really. He just has this roundabout way of telling me that I need to relax and let things happen when they happen."

Jacobi stayed silent, just listening.

"I wanted to ask you if he's said anything to you."

*Here we go...* Jacobi never liked being caught in the middle of those two.

"Not really," she tried to keep from lying to her. "I mean, I know the miscarriages were just as hard on him. I do think he's worried about putting you through too much again."

"I was hoping you would talk to him for me."

"As in convince him?"

"Maybe."

"Marti, I don't know..."

"You are his best friend. He listens to you. Just try, okay? I don't know, pick his brain and see what he's not sharing with me. Is this about more than his genuine concern for me?"

Jacobi stayed silent for longer than she should have. There was more, and she knew the real reason why Ben did not want to have another child. She didn't simply know because they constantly confided in each other. It was because the two of them had deep, rooted feelings for each other. Feelings that neither of them should ever allow to resurface.

"I'll talk to him," Jacobi finally agreed.

"Oh wonderful! Thanks, Cobi."

"You're welcome. I should go now."

# Chapter 4

She had never done anything like this before, but Jacobi knew they needed privacy. She was still on her lunch break and unsure if Ben was occupied with seeing patients. Unlike herself, as she kept her cell phone in her locker, Ben always had his in his pant pocket. Partly, he claimed, he had gotten into the habit of that when his wife was pregnant.

Jacobi's text to him felt wrong on so many levels, but she sent it anyway. She didn't want to give him mixed signals, but she did realize that her words could have done just that once her message was already sent.

*Meet me in Exam Room 3.*

## Nothing Left to Give

Jacobi was already in there, with the door closed for privacy, when she noticed the doorhandle turn. Ben stepped inside and quickly shut the door behind him. He looked at her from across the room. She was sitting on the edge of the exam table, her feet dangling. Today her black scrubs were nearly as dark as her hair. And she still wore those white comfort shoes on her feet with no-show socks.

Ben always wore the standard aqua blue scrubs. He preferred those and Jacobi giggled at the routine of his uniform. The only thing he switched about were the tennis shoes on his feet. The man was obsessed with having a grand shoe collection.

"Why did you call me in here?" he asked her, stepping into the middle of the room.

"To talk. To get this, whatever this is between us that you suddenly felt the need to wave in my face, out in the open. I want to know what you want. For God's sake, Marti senses that you are keeping something from her."

Ben's eyes widened. "What? The two of you have talked about this?"

"What exactly is *this*?" she referenced again.

"Us," he clarified.

"There is no us, Ben. You and I are friends and colleagues. That's all we can ever be. Think of Marti and Suzie. Please."

He disregarded her plea. "What does Marti know?"

"Nothing that I've shared with her," Jacobi clarified. "She asked me to talk to you about having another baby. I guess she senses that your whole heart isn't in it."

"That's because it's not."

"Try, Ben."

"I can't live a lie. Marti deserves better than that. We all do."

"What exactly does that even mean? You're leaving her? Jesus, Ben. Focus on being a father. Who the hell wants shared custody and missed moments? You all belong under the same roof, living as a family."

"Suzie will always have me by her side when she needs me. She will know that forever. I am thinking of you. And us. I want the chance that we never took. It's our turn, or at least it's our chance to take it."

Jacobi hopped off the exam table and landed hard on her feet. She wanted to grab him by the shoulders and shake some sense into him. "I never agreed to anything that you are drumming up in that senseless head of yours. Stay with your wife. Raise a family with her."

She watched Ben shake his head adamantly. His dark hair was a little longer than he typically kept it. It was wavy and a tad curlier in spots, like around his ears. "Just stop for a moment. Put Marti and Suzie out of your head." Jacobi began to object, but before she could speak, he shushed her and continued speaking. "You and I share everything, a passion for this job, a friendship that runs deep. You are my person, Reese Jacobi. I want more. I want to stretch the boundaries. I know we can be even better together. I can feel it."

"We've already blown past those boundaries," she tried to remind him without falling victim again to that vivid, intense memory of the night they shared together. "We've had sex, Ben. Is that what you want from me again? Some sort of affair? I don't understand. And, quite frankly, I have nothing left to give."

The accuracy of her own statement left Jacobi at a loss for more words. She didn't have anything left to give him or anyone else. It hurt too much either way.

"I don't see it that way at all."

"You're being selfish," she accused him.

"Maybe so, but at least I know what I want. At least I'm not lying to myself."

His words instantly angered her. "I am not lying to myself. I am keeping my feelings to myself. There's a fucking difference!"

"What feelings? Now, Jacobi. Now is the time for you to admit what kind of feelings are in your heart."

She tried to move away from him. She wasn't ready to open the door of that private room and leave. Not yet. But she did need to put some distance between herself and him. He grabbed her by the shoulders. He made her look at him.

"You want to know what's in my heart?" she actually laughed a little at what he was asking of her. "I love you, Ben. There was an instantaneous ease between us and that has never wavered. We share chemistry, trust, and comfort. We have big dreams of one day starting up our own practice together. I love your wife like a sister, and your little girl like my own. The three of you are my family. You don't mess with unbreakable bonds like that. You don't purposely crack something so solid and then watch it spread until it's destroyed. I don't have it in me to ever be that selfish, and you shouldn't either. Not for anything."

"I've spent the last five years playing by those rules," he responded. "I'm out of patience with myself. I see you here, day in and day out. I pick your brain about medical things, I get glimpses of your private life, but then I have to watch you leave. *See you tomorrow* just isn't enough anymore. I want to know what you do at night, when you're alone, if you're alone. I can't handle knowing if someone else is lying beside you… touching you."

"Please. Don't."

Ben again ignored her plea. He placed his open palm on her face… just like he did all those years ago the first time they kissed in his apartment the night before his wedding. She closed her eyes and felt a tear escape down her cheek. He brushed that tear away with his thumb. "This hurts me, too," he told her, "but we need each other. You know that's true. If you don't, if you disagree, I'll back off and we can resume being who everyone believes us to be."

She stayed quiet.

"Tell me to stop, and I will."

She looked away from him. She was annoyed with herself for feeling weak. And for crying in front of him. "I can't."

He leaned closer to her, and she didn't resist him in her space. It suddenly became too much effort to deny her heart any longer. Their eyes met. Their lips touched, softly and tenderly. Their bodies were practically sealed together now. They deepened their kiss as Ben gently backed her against the exam table. They kissed long. And hard. And their emotions intensified. She ran her fingers through his hair as he pressed his hand to the small of her arched back. She lifted her leg, wrapping it around his waist. He stifled a chuckle with his lips still on hers. There was no one like Jacobi. She was fun, spontaneous, and extremely sensual. Ben reacted by pressing his erection into her lower belly.

They had to stop. Now. Any moment either one of them could be paged, or a knock could sound on the other side of that door. Or worse, someone could walk in on them. They had staff and patients looking for them and waiting for them. The last thing they also needed was for someone to catch on. To see her face that clearly had to be flushed, or to notice his disheveled hair.

Jacobi pushed him away with both hands on his chest.

"We can't do this."

"Right. Not here."

"I need to gather myself, find my bearings or something, before I step out that door. And, I have to go into that hallway alone. Stay back for a few minutes. God, what we're doing in here is incredibly unprofessional." And wrong. She could not forget that it was just plain wrong.

"Go. We won't let this happen again here. I just needed to know, to be sure. You want to be with me, too."

"What I want is to be strong enough to tell you that you're mistaken."

He smiled at her.

"Damn you," she uttered under her breath and abruptly left him standing in there alone.

# Chapter 5

It happened every time he came home from work at a decent hour. He heard the pitter patter of little feet on the hardwood flooring in their house. And when she saw him, she squealed as he'd chase her and then swoop her up into his arms. Suzie adored her daddy, and that incredible feeling was mutual. Ben couldn't imagine not being in his little girl's life full-time, but leaving her mother would have to happen sooner than later. If he wanted to be with Jacobi, he needed to end his marriage. Neither one of them were looking to have an affair, to lie, or to cheat. Marti deserved better than that. She had a right to know the truth.

Ben held his little girl close to his chest. He kissed the wild blonde curls on top her head.

"Daddy, play with me."

"I sure will. I just need to change my clothes first, okay?" Ben set her back on her feet on the floor, and she ran off, likely directly to her toys.

Ben saw Marti leaning against the door frame between the kitchen and the living room. "Hey you," she smiled. She was pretty, and typically such a confident woman.

"Hi. How was your day?"

"Good, but my night is going to be better," she winked at him.

Ben creased his brow. "Oh yeah? What's going on tonight?"

"I used my ovulation kit this morning. It needs to happen tonight. I would drag you upstairs right now if Suzie was napping. I've been trying to get her to go down for the last hour."

Ben was quiet. There was no way that he could make love to his wife. He couldn't risk that chance of actually getting her pregnant. He all but shook his head at himself for having that thought, as there was a lengthy period of time when both of them wished to conceive every single time they tried.

"I have a good feeling about this. I mean, remaining positive is part of the success of anything, right?"

Ben nodded. "Right."

"So, seriously, go get changed and play while I finish up dinner. We're all going to bed early tonight!" she giggled, and Ben turned his back to her and headed for the stairway.

~

## Nothing Left to Give

Ben was last to tuck Suzie into bed. Marti had already read her a bedtime story, when he came in her room, knelt by her toddler bed, and kissed her goodnight on her forehead. "I love you, Sooz."

"I love you, daddy." Her little voice melted his heart every time. Her Ls were pronounced as Ws, and it was the most precious thing he had ever heard.

Ben closed her door and walked across the hallway to the bedroom that he shared with his wife. Marti was already in bed, well, more like she was sitting on the bed in a red negligée that left very little to his imagination. She was sexy; he just didn't want her anymore. He felt like less of a person for feeling that way, but his bond with Jacobi was stronger and deeper than anything he had ever known in his life. He could no longer deny that he wanted another woman in place of her.

"Drop your pants, buddy. I'm running out of patience."

He forced a chuckle. "Can we not rush this?" he asked her.

"Seriously? I'm telling you that I want sex, and I want it now, and you're thinking about taking your time? Are you even a man?" She laughed out loud.

"I'm sorry, I'm just distracted, or tired, I guess. Long day."

"You can be asleep in ten minutes. Come on, Ben. We have to do this tonight."

He didn't respond.

"Is something wrong?"

"We need to talk," were the only words he thought to reply. To stop her from pushing him to have sex.

"Oh my God, later, okay? I'll listen to you talk all night long. Just get in bed with me right now and let's do it."

"Is this really how you want to conceive a child together? Where's the passion and the love?"

"What do you mean? I'm turned on as hell right now, and I love you, you know that."

He did. And he loved her, too. But he was not in love with her. Not anymore.

His cell phone sounded on the dresser top. The tone was his emergency page. Marti bounced to her knees on the bed. "No! There is no damn way that you have an emergency call right now. Tell that woman in labor to hold the baby in. Please!"

Ben was quick to get to his phone. He looked at the screen, and then back at his wife. "I have to go to the hospital."

He watched her hustle to get off the bed and to get to him. Her breasts were spilling out overtop all that lace. "Wait five minutes. That's all I need. I will give you a blowjob, and you just need to finish inside me the moment you get close."

"Jesus, Marti!" Ben backed away from her. "You're desperate and I can't take anymore of it." He distanced himself from her and never looked back when he walked out of their bedroom.

He slipped into his shoes downstairs and grabbed his car keys and wallet off the counter. Before he backed his car out of the driveway, he looked down at his phone on the passenger seat. The message repeated on his screen again. It was just a test, a run through of the paging system. There had been a few glitches lately, and tonight was just a mock test to be sure the messages were going through. Ben knew that upstairs in their bedroom, but he used it as an opportunity to escape his wife and the demand that he just could not fill.

∼

Three miles away, he drove to Jacobi's condo. There was nowhere else for him to turn. No one else that he wanted to be with more.

He parked his car on her driveway and walked up to the front door and rang the bell. He never gave her a warning that he was dropping by after dark. He would explain himself when he saw her.

She opened the door wearing a sports bra and leggings. Her feet were bare, and her hair was pulled up in a knot on top her head.

"What in the hell?" That was her way of asking him what he was doing there.

"I should have called or sent a quick text. It looks like I'm interrupting your workout."

"Yes, on both accounts," she told him, as she studied his face. "You didn't just leave Marti, did you? Does she know?" She refrained from saying, *about us*, because really, that still seemed surreal. And wrong. She reminded herself of that every few minutes it seemed.

Ben shook his head, and then looked down at his feet on the concrete.

"Come inside."

He stepped into her house. A barre sculpting YouTube video was paused on the flat screen TV mounted high on the wall.

"Sit down and tell me what happened." She sat on a chair adjacent to the sofa where Ben was while he explained everything that happened with Marti tonight. He spared no details, including his escape from the house after feigning an emergency page.

"Goodness," Jacobi reacted. "She's desperate."

"Yeah, I know," Ben shook his head. "It's sad, really. And I know if we were not interrupted by the hospital, I would have told her the truth about how I feel, or don't feel anymore."

"That sickens me, Ben. You are going to hurt her so badly."

He quietly nodded. "I don't mean to. I just can't live this way any longer."

"You shouldn't be here."

"I didn't have anywhere else to go."

"I'm not going to sleep with you. Don't come here wanting to get into my bed. It's not right. You still have a wife."

"I'll go home, eventually. I just need the storm to blow over."

"There's always going to be a next time until you're honest with her, but I don't know if you should be completely forthright with her, if you know what I mean."

"If she knows how we feel about each other, she is going to automatically believe that it's been going on all along, a never-ending affair or something sordid."

"I'm going to lose her, too," Jacobi sighed. "I don't want things to change like that. I still need my friend… and little Suzie in my life. It's just all such a huge sacrifice."

"Are you saying that you're having second thoughts about us?"

"I haven't even had time to process my initial thoughts about any of this! You're the one who sprung this all on me."

"Stop acting like what's between us just happened. It's always been there, rooted deep. We just finally chose to admit it."

"Because you wouldn't let up."

"I don't think you're sorry about that. Are you?" he winked at her.

She tried to smile at him. "I can keep my feelings hid. Clearly, I have for a very long time."

"We shouldn't have to sacrifice how we feel. Not anymore. Jacobi, we have one chance in this life to be truly happy and neither one of us have seized it. I don't know about you, but I'm done. I want you to allow us to be more to each other than what we already are. That's saying a lot, you know? Because you already mean the world to me."

She closed her eyes and clasped her hands on her lap, and when she opened them again, he was at her feet. From his knees on the hardwood flooring, he placed his hands on top of hers. "I love you differently than I've ever loved anyone else. For so long, our lives have been intertwined. The night that we gave into our attraction, to the love that we've always shared, we swore that was all it could ever be. Well, we were wrong. Something that feels so right should not have to be suppressed or hidden. Ever."

Jacobi fought tears. "We are going to hurt people. Can we really be that selfish?"

"Aren't we both hurting now? It's painful for me not to be with you, to reach for you and hold you. Can you honestly say that you don't feel the same?"

She halfheartedly smiled at him through her tears. The tears that she had not been able to wipe off her face because he was still holding her hands in his. "If you only knew the feelings I've kept inside."

"I'm sorry," he spoke sincerely. "It could not have been easy for you to watch me marry someone else… and start a family. You've been so much a part of all that. Our lives are connected from every angle, and always will be. I just want more. I can't help it. Tell me that you do too."

She was still crying when she took her hands from his and placed them on both sides of his face. "I shouldn't feel this way, but I do. It's wrong, yet it feels right. You walked in here tonight and I told you that you couldn't stay, that I wouldn't sleep with you because you're married. But when you're this close, touching me, looking at me like that... I completely lose all my senses. Suddenly, we're not doctors. You're not someone else's husband. We are simply you and me. Two alike hearts. Two souls that found each other a long time ago. I need to be with you, too, Ben. I physically ache for you."

She met him halfway. Their kiss exploded with intensity and desire. He heard her whimper, and he gave her all that he had of himself. He pulled and twisted her fitted sports bra over her head. He touched her bare breasts, then her nipples with his fingers, those delicate hands of a surgeon, and then with his mouth. She tore off his shirt and forced down his pants. He peeled off her leggings that she was wearing sans underwear. They made their way down to the hardwood floor. There was no waiting. The bedroom was too far away at this moment. He touched her between her legs, and she moaned aloud. God, it had been too long since she felt this way with him. "Now. Ben." She urged him to drop his boxers, which he kicked off at his ankles. Down on his knees, on the floor again, she reached for him. Stroked him. There was an urgent need to be inside her. She felt the same rush as he plunged himself between her legs and filled her. No other man had ever fit so well. Jacobi came undone as he thrusted inside her once, twice, and a then a third time. Harder. Deeper. Her body shook with a sudden, explosive release, as he watched her and pushed into her, again and again, until he too found an earth-shattering release. They were naked in each other's arms, still touching and feeling their bodies in the most intimate way. It felt surreal to be together like this after all that time.

Still mid afterglow, she led him to her bedroom, where they made love slower and more attentively. He savored her, every inch of her. She drove him to the brink, doing things to him that he longed for with only her hands and her mouth. And just a few hours later, they had to say goodbye again.

# Chapter 6

It was after midnight when Ben went home. He slept on the sofa in the living room to avoid waking Marti or sleeping in the same bed with her. Being with Jacobi again had changed things. There was no going back now.

Suzie was in her highchair eating scrambled eggs when Ben got out of the shower and made his way downstairs to the kitchen. Marti was the first to speak once he greeted his little girl with kisses on top of her blonde curls that were wildly rearranged all over her head from sleeping.

"You slept on the sofa after you came home," Marti noted.

He nodded, while he made fleeting eye contact from her to their daughter.

"It would have been nice to know that you made it home." Gone were the days when he would carefully slip into bed, no matter what hour, and spoon her body with his own as he fell asleep. Sometimes Marti didn't fully wake up, but subconsciously she had known he was home and beside her again.

Marti sensed his tension and she needed to make things right between them. They both focused on Suzie and only talking to her while she ate her breakfast and then wanted out of her highchair to run to her toys in the living room. Once she was settled, Marti sat down at the table. Ben stared at his coffee, while he traced the rim of the mug with his index finger.

"Ben," she broke the awkward silence between them. "About last night... I'm sorry. I was so desperate, and I realize that I overwhelmed you."

He looked at her, really looked at her, for the first time this morning. "It was definitely too much," he agreed, and he refrained from saying that it wasn't just her behavior for one night that she needed to get in check with. The mere idea of wanting to have another baby had consumed her for a very long time.

"Was Jacobi with you last night?"

Ben jerked his head in her direction. "What?"

"Jacobi? Was she called in last night with you at the hospital?"

He caught his breath and tried to relax. He was guilty as sin, but her question had actually been a typical, innocent one. "Yeah, um, we both had deliveries. Why?"

"Well I was worried about you, and I regretted how I acted before you left in such a hurry, so I texted her. When I didn't hear back, I assumed she was working as well."

Ben nodded. So much about their lives would change. Even the close friendship between Marti and Jacobi would end. And it wouldn't end well.

"Right. I've told you that she doesn't even carry her phone on her at the hospital. Most of us do, but hers is always tucked away in her locker."

"It's so fun how you two know all those little things about each other," Marti smiled. "I mean, how could you not? Through the years you both have remained close. I love that she's a big part of my life and Suzie's too."

Ben forced a smile. What the hell else was he supposed to do at this point?

"She really needs to find a man. Not just one to grab dinner with or have a brief fling."

Ben now felt uncomfortable. "I'm sure Jacobi knows what she's doing with her own life."

"She's 35 years old. Believe me, women want more in their lives by then." Marti was only casually speaking, but Ben suddenly felt the need to break his silence.

"Sometimes life doesn't work out the way we think it should, or the way we really want it to," Ben chose his words carefully.

"Please don't say that you want to wait to try for another baby. I need you to be as ready as I am, and I feel like you were ready several months ago. I mean, before we lost two…" her voice trailed off.

"Do you even hear yourself? Nothing has changed since last night. You apologize over and over, but I don't think you are genuinely sorry. Not when you jump right back into this act of desperation. I'm done with it."

"What do you mean you're done with it?"

Ben's eyes bore into hers. "I think we need to take a break."

"You've said that and I've heard you; I have. I guess we can wait a month or two before trying again, if that's what you really believe is best as a doctor and as my husband."

That was just it. He didn't want to be her *husband* anymore.

"This isn't just about getting pregnant," he told her, directly, yet cautiously. I mean, us. I've been struggling with this for a while, and I'm at a crossroad where I have nothing left to give."

Marti wore a look of utter confusion on her face. "You're what? Nothing left to give me? Our marriage? I don't even know what you're saying to me."

It broke his heart to spring such a devastating shock on her. If she had paid attention, though, she would have picked up on the signs. Or perhaps she had? Things just had not been the same between them. The strain of getting pregnant and losing two babies had done them both in, in very different ways. They certainly drifted apart, with Marti being the one to choose to be oblivious to it. Unfortunately, her notorious way of only seeing what she wanted to see was going to make this all the more difficult. Ben definitely felt like the bad guy, and he dreaded her reaction when she learned of him and Jacobi. She would naturally believe that Jacobi was to blame, that she had crossed the boundaries of their friendship and stolen her husband. It was Ben though. He and Jacobi had a history of close friendship and one, one night stand. It was him who wanted more now. He was tired of fighting for a marriage that was no longer working. What he shared with Jacobi was what he wanted to nourish and fight for.

"I'm sorry," he told her. "Suzie is, and always will be, my first priority. She will never doubt that, but, I want out of our marriage."

Marti threw her hands up in the air and pushed her chair back so hard on the floor that it likely had scratched the hardwood flooring underneath. Those chair legs made a screeching sound. A sound similar to car tires coming to an abrupt halt. A forced stop. Ironically, that was symbolic to what Ben had done to their marriage. His decision to stop being her husband would likely leave lasting scars. "Where is this coming from? Do you really think it works that way? My God, Ben! Couples have issues all the time, but they talk about it... they work it out. We could see a therapist if that's what you need, or better yet, talk to Jacobi. She has always been your voice of reason. Mine too, for that matter. You can't just spontaneously leave!"

Ben completely heard her out before he responded. "Our marriage is broken, whether you can see it or not. It can't be fixed. You and I are like glass, we're strong but fragile. We break and those cracks remain. It's reached a point for me where I'm tired of getting hurt from the shards when I try to piece us back together."

"I've hurt you?" her tone was snarky. "How? By reeling from the pain of losing our babies? For wanting a family with you?"

A little voice from the other room interrupted them. "Daddy? Come see!"

Ben stood up.

"No! We are not done here!"

"She's calling me. I am going to her." The irritation was evident in his voice. This wasn't the first time that Marti's selfishness trumped everything, including Suzie's needs.

Ben took his time sitting down on the floor, interacting, and playing with his little girl. He was in no hurry to get back into the kitchen and face his wife's wrath. He was expecting the shock to have somewhat worn off, and the anger and the bargaining to begin. And when he returned to her, he was right.

"Is there someone else?" her eyes were red, and her cheeks were blotchy. Clearly, she had been crying. "Are you sleeping with another woman?"

"My decision to leave is about us. I love you, Marti, but I am not in love with you."

She stifled a sob, and his own guilt was about to do him in as well. "You can find your way back. I will do anything to remind you of how good we are together. I swear to God, Ben. If you only want one child, that's what we'll have. Yes, I badly want another one, but I can make that sacrifice for you. For us! Just don't give up. Stay. Please." She walked up to him, standing in the open entrance between the living room and the kitchen. She placed her hands on both sides of his face. She pressed her lips to his, forcing him to respond. But he didn't.

He took ahold of her wrists, gently, with his own hands. He slowly shook his head. He didn't want to hurt her. He knew her so well, though. He couldn't give her any hope at all, because she would cling to it and never let go. "Nothing will change things between us. There's no amount of words or actions anymore. No out-of-reach promises. No pleading. No makeup sex. None of that will change anything. This is where it ends, Marti."

# Chapter 7

Jacobi hadn't been able to get a word in. She didn't ask where Suzie was, or if Ben was taking care of her, or what was going on. Marti was standing at Jacobi's door after she had just finished pulling her hair up, applying a little foundation and mascara to her face, and slipping on her scrubs for the day.

They were seated in Jacobi's kitchen, where she had offered Marti a cup of coffee. Her words were still ringing in Jacobi's ears.

*Ben wants to leave me. He said it's over. He's not in love with me anymore.*

Clearly, Ben had left out the part of them turning to each other last night. Jacobi didn't like herself very much right now, as Marti chose to confide in her during her weakest moment. *What kind of friend betrayed another?*

"I know he's been upset or annoyed with me and my obsession with wanting to try for another baby. I told him that I would stop. I'll give up, we'll only have Suzie, and just be happy all together. I begged him." Marti's words were incoherent as she began crying again. Jacobi reached for her hand on the table, searching for the words to say to her.

"I know that has taken a toll on both of you," she was careful to say.

"To the point of ending our marriage, though? I mean, I just feel like there's more. There has to be." Jacobi felt the tension rise in her chest. "I asked him if he's cheating on me."

Jacobi let go of her hand. She could no longer pretend. She imagined that Ben had chosen to keep the whole truth from his wife to protect her, or himself, or even Jacobi and the friendship they shared. But that was wrong.

"I feel like there is no easy way to tell you what you deserve to know," Jacobi cautiously spoke. "I want to ask you to keep your butt in that chair until I'm finished speaking. Hear my words before you react. I mean it, Marti. Can you do that?"

"You know something!" Marti already began to impatiently react.

Jacobi reminded her, "I want you to hear me out."

"Okay fine. Just tell me!" Marti's nervousness escalated.

"When Ben and I met, we connected as medical students, and almost instantly we became close friends. He was my person. His family, you and Suzie, are my family too."

"He has always been able to confide in you. I know that," Marti blindly supported their relationship.

"Marti, please just let me say this. I've never tried to explain this before." There was evident pain on Jacobi's face, and that did not go unnoticed. "Just listen to me."

Marti conceded, kept silent, and nodded her head.

"I've never found anyone to share my life with because I don't want to know that feeling with someone else." Marti's facial expression shifted as she began to grasp Jacobi's words. "The night before your wedding, I drove Ben back to his apartment. We were drinking and talking about life. We weren't falling-down drunk, probably just tipsy. We knew what we were doing, and we made a pact to never tell anyone. We wanted to be closer than we've ever been. We slept together before he married you."

"That was five years ago," Marti choked out the words. "Am I really supposed to believe that you haven't screwed my husband since? I feel like such a fool," she went on talking. "I've seen the way you two are bonded. I've had other friends ask me who you were. *Who is that woman talking to Ben?* I yielded those inquiries at my own wedding. *Oh that's my husband's best friend. She's an OBGYN, too. We love her like a sister!"*

Jacobi momentarily looked down at her hands folded together on the tabletop. "We put that night behind us. We never looked back. He was your husband all these years, trying to make you happy and be happy himself."

"What is that supposed to mean? We have been happy together. Tell me, if the two of you had your one-night stand out of curiosity or just a good time, why are you admitting the truth to me now? What changed?" Marti already feared the answer to her own question.

"Ben recently had a change of heart about staying in your marriage. I was just as surprised to hear it as you; believe me. I've encouraged him to stay with you and fight for your family. You both have Suzie to think about. I don't want to see her life change, or any of yours."

"Then talk to him."

"I tried."

"Tell him that you don't want anything to change between you and him. Tell him that you can't take the risk of losing your fucking friendship!" Marti lashed out in desperation, mocking their bond. "Make him understand that your one-night stand is in the past, where it needs to stay."

"He came to me last night," Jacobi practically blurted out those words. "I don't know how else to say this, other than to just tell you the truth. We can no longer fight what's between us. It's more than two medical minds feeding off each other. And it's so much more than friendship."

"He came to you? So, he showed up here for moral support? Or, was my husband in your bed again?"

Jacobi never ceased eye contact with Marti while she nodded her head.

"You're not even sorry, are you?"

"I should be. I know I should be. But I love him. I've always loved him."

"But he was mine first!"

"No," Jacobi quietly objected. "Our souls knew each other before you."

"Soul mates? He's *my* husband, the father of my little girl. Doesn't that mean anything to you?"

"Of course it does. And, if Ben changed his mind and wanted to try again to piece his family back together, I would let him go. This time, though, that's not what he wants. And, honestly, I no longer have the strength to walk away or to just step aside again. I already let him go once, the day that I watched him marry you."

"I'm not you," Marti reacted. "I don't want to back down or falsify my feelings. I can actually live with knowing the two of you have had sex. What I can't live without is Ben."

This was unexpected at the very least. Jacobi had been sitting there, speaking the truth she had buried for so long, all while she was preparing for Marti to come undone. *Isn't that what girlfriends did when one found out that the other betrayed them?* "I anticipated being on the receiving end of your wrath right now," Jacobi admitted, not knowing if she should be confused or grateful. "I imagined having to defend myself. I didn't plan for this. I didn't purposely take him away from you."

"It's me, Cobi. I'm not like everyone else. I am hurt and I'm angry, but the wheels in my mind are spinning and searching for a way to hold onto what I have. I need Ben. You are the complete opposite of me. You are strong and independent, and you can always power through anything."

## Nothing Left to Give

"It's what I want people to perceive," Jacobi admitted, "but I am human, and I know what hurt feels like."

"Do you remember when Suzie was born, and I had that meltdown about needing to always give her two parents? You wholeheartedly agreed with me. I felt like we shared something in common, both coming from divorced parents and broken families."

Marti's story was vastly different than Jacobi's. Jacobi's parents divorced when she was 11 years old, and her brother was 8. Both their mother and father split amicably and remained friends. There was never a negative word spoken about the other to their children. It was a lesson learned for Jacobi as a child; sometimes people were happier apart. Marti's parents, however, went through a nasty divorce when Marti and her older sister were teenagers. Marti's mother ultimately reeled from the split.

"You're right. I never wanted that for Suzie," Jacobi agreed.

"My mother lost her mind when my father walked out."

Jacobi sat up straighter and boldly reached for Marti's hands on the table with her own. She gripped them tightly, fearing that she would pull away. "You listen to me. You are not your mother. What she did altered your entire life. You hated her for it for a very long time. Do not, I mean it, Marti, do not ever hurt Suzie that way."

There were tears in Marti's eyes. She held onto Jacobi's hands. "That's just it. I never thought I'd have a reason in my life to feel unstable or desperate. This morning, at the house, that kind of hopelessness consumed me when Ben said he wanted out of our marriage. I can't watch him leave. I was so afraid that he would just wear the clothes on his back and not return to our house after work. I ran out. He tried to stop me and reason with me. *He had to be at work this morning. What about Suzie?* I backed my car out of our driveway so fast. I didn't know where I would go, but I could not be the one to watch him leave me. I wasn't even thinking about my child. What kind of mother does that? Mine did. And here I am, not so unlike her after all."

"That's not true and you know it! Despite the excuse… that she was not in her right frame of mind… your mother was a coward. You are not her, Marti. You have so many reasons to live. You are still young and beautiful and smart and the most headstrong person I've ever met in my life. Use that stubbornness and determination to push yourself through the hardships. You have your little girl to focus on, to love, and to live for."

Marti was openly crying. "I should hate you right now," she sobbed. Marti stared at Jacobi and there was more pain on her face than anger. "You're the reason I'm going to lose him. Yet, here I am, listening to your words of wisdom because Jacobi knows exactly what to say, she always has all the answers. Well, guess what, you are the only one who can fix this for me. Don't give Ben a chance. Give him back to me."

Jacobi felt sickened and the tears welled up in her own eyes. "I've tried," she answered. "That's not what he wants. You need to understand that this isn't just about me, or you. Ben's feelings mean something, too. He's made up his mind. I'm so sorry that you had to get caught in the crossfire of something that's always been between him and I. It's unfair to you. We both love you, Marti."

"But you love each other more."

# Chapter 8

Jacobi was eight minutes late for work. She barreled down the hallway and into her office, but not without bumping into everyone's favorite OB nurse, Reeda.

"It's not like you to be late," she was quick to point out. "Aren't you the one who lives by the gospel truth of arriving everywhere at least ten minutes early?" She was teasing her, of course, but Jacobi's nonreaction caused a little alarm. "I hope everything is alright."

"I'm fine. I'm sure I have a patient waiting on me though."

"Room 5. You'll find the single, first-time momma whose baby daddy came along with her today."

"Oh," Jacobi noted. "Thanks for the heads up."

"One more thing," Reeda caught Jacobi as she had already taken more than a few steps away from her. "Dr. Oliver seems to be running late as well; only, he called. He'll be here as soon as he can."

"Does he want me to squeeze in a patient or two of his, if I can?"

Reeda shrugged. "You may have to."

"Okay, let me know," was all Jacobi said, as it was nothing new for the two of them to cover for each other.

"I do find it odd that two of the promptest people in the universe were both late arrivals on the same morning," Reeda spoke aloud as she kept her back to Jacobi and continued walking.

"Happenstance!" Jacobi called out to her, also without looking back.

~

Ben arrived soon after Jacobi and immediately saw his first patient almost thirty minutes past her scheduled appointment time. Throughout the day, Jacobi only saw him in the hallway, in passing. Now, she had just given him a fleeting glance as she intended to move past the open doorway of his office unseen. But he looked up and saw her. Before he could call her name and summon her back there, Jacobi sped up her pace and entered her own office adjacent to his.

They never had the chance to talk privately about what transpired between her and Marti this morning. *Had he known that Jacobi told Marti everything?* She sat down at her desk and sighed. She couldn't work like this. She needed to stay focused. And there he was now, standing in her open doorway.

"Can I come in?"

"No," she answered him, and he chuckled under his breath and walked through the doorway regardless. He sat down on the corner of her desk, directly in front of her. That was nothing new, but the way the pant leg of his scrubs hiked up and revealed the dark hair on his leg had her mind flashing back to his whole body against hers last night. She forced that memory away. That was, after all, what she did best.

"I know that Marti went to see you this morning when she rushed out," Ben got right to the point of the conversation that they needed to have. But Jacobi wasn't sure of this being the right time or place to get into anything about the mess they'd made of all their lives.

"How much else do you know?"

"You told her about us." His face was momentarily expressionless and impossible to read. It was pointless for him to be angry anyway. What was said and done was over.

"I had to," Jacobi defended herself. "She came to me for support. I couldn't lie to her. Since you went as far as telling her that you want out of your marriage, I believed she deserved to know why."

"I don't want her to blame you. Our marriage isn't working for other reasons, too."

"As unbelievable as it may seem, she didn't lash out at me; she doesn't seem to hate me," Jacobi declared. "She does expect me to change your mind though. She wants me to give you back to her." Jacobi sighed, and when she looked up at him, her dark eyes looked dazed. "The thing is, you're not mine. You're Marti's husband."

"Do I have a say so here? I am a grown man, capable of making my own decisions."

"There was a time when you loved her, and you chose to spend your life with her," Jacobi was quick to remind him. The truth was, she saw Ben going back to his wife and resuming his life with her and their child as the easiest way out of this. Less people would be hurt.

"I don't want to cause anyone pain," he kept his voice low because the door was open and any moment there could be foot traffic in there. "But we both know it's our turn, and if we don't seize it, that will be the worst regret from all of this."

She gave him a soft smile. *This time, he chose her.*

"I know you feel the same," his eyes bore into hers.

"Sorry to interrupt the consultation, doctors, but you each have a patient waiting in those unflattering paper gowns. Let's not torture them any longer than necessary." They laughed in unison, while Reeda stifled a giggle behind her wide smile. She liked to think of herself as perceptive. Something had certainly appeared to be different, being around them, at that hospital, in recent days.

~

When Jacobi closed the door to the exam room, leaving her final patient of the day, she heard voices down the hallway at the nurse's station. She kept walking in that direction even after she knew who was there. The nurses were gathered and doting over two-year-old Suzie, and Marti stood back, confident and smiling, as if nothing at all had changed in her world. As Jacobi was only a few steps away, the little one spotted her. Suddenly all the attention from the nurses was insignificant. "Cobi!" She ran to her as quickly as those toddler legs would allow her to move. Jacobi swooped her up in her arms and spun her around. She held her close and pressed her nose into those full blonde curls.

"What brings you two here?" Jacobi's question was directed at Marti. They shared a look. It was as if Marti was feigning some sort of air of overconfidence. Jacobi played along. If she was upset after all, Jacobi was not about to meet her anger with anger.

"We wanted to see daddy, didn't we, Sooz?"

As if on cue, Ben rounded the corner and momentarily stopped when he saw them. Suzie leaned from Jacobi's arms toward him. Ben's face lit up when he reached for her, as his hand brushed against Jacobi's.

"Why did you come to see daddy at work?" Ben phrased the question to Suzie but looked at his wife.

"We were close by, running errands, and we wanted to surprise you."

"I like surprises," Ben smiled, focusing his attention on Suzie, while all eyes were on him and his family. His life certainly didn't feel as perfect as it appeared from the outside.

"If you're done here soon, let's grab some dinner," Marti suggested, as she was overheard by half the staff on the OB floor of Cleveland Clinic. She wanted it that way. That's why they came there. She was making a point, a statement. *This is my husband, and we are a family.*

"Follow me to my office and we'll figure that out," Ben told Marti while the nurses took turns waving at Suzie and telling her goodbye. Jacobi stepped over to the main desk, attempting to busy herself while the three of them walked down the hallway together. As a family. That truth stung now more than ever. She and Ben had crossed a line that was going to forever change things, but it was quite clear that Marti wasn't going to give up on him.

"That's a precious thing right there. A family like that. The Lord certainly has blessed them abundantly." Reeda's declaration didn't help Jacobi's guilty mindset right now. She only smiled in response and then promptly made her way to her own office. Whether she had work to do or not, she was going to sit in there until the Oliver family left the building.

# Chapter 9

Ben was quick to distract Suzie with a basket of mini board books that he had been meaning to bring home to her. Sellers were always promoting their products to be on display in the hospital waiting rooms. Those tiny books were free samples from a few days ago. As he expected, Suzie was immediately intrigued with them. She was sitting on the floor at his feet when Marti walked around his desk and sat down on his chair.

He looked at her from across the room. He stepped a little closer to the desk and away from Suzie. She was too little to comprehend a serious conversation between her parents, and that was precisely what they were about to have.

"What was that all about?" Ben asked Marti.

She shrugged her shoulders. "It's not like your family hasn't stopped in unannounced before."

Her way of emphasizing words like *your family* hadn't gone unnoticed to him. "We need to talk, but not here. I don't know why you couldn't wait another hour or so before I made it home."

"Maybe I wasn't sure that you were going to come home."

Before Ben responded, he looked at Suzie, still very much interested in flipping the hard pages of the books that were just the right size for her small palms. He was only thinking of her right now, and how he would never just not come home to be with her. He was her daddy. "That's not fair."

"No? Why don't you tell me what is fair then, because it feels pretty damn unfair to find out that you weren't in my bed last night because you were with her."

While Ben felt a sense of relief knowing that Marti knew the truth about him and Jacobi, it still didn't make it easier to muster the words to explain himself. That was just it, he didn't have a way to make this sound better or to deem it as acceptable. He was in love with Jacobi. That was his truth. And there didn't seem to be a way for Marti to grasp that. He understood being to blame for her shock and her sorrow, but what unnerved him was that she appeared to be in complete denial. It was as if she was expecting him to beg for her forgiveness, so they could move past this inconvenient disruption to their lives. Her showing up there, at the hospital where he worked alongside Jacobi, was Marti's way of claiming her stake. She had invested everything into her marriage and creating a family with him, and Ben knew all too well that she was not about to back down.

"I'm sorry," was all he said.

"I know," she answered, as if she was ready to forgive and forget so they could move past this — together.

"Don't turn this around, Marti. I feel awful being the one to end our marriage, and I'm apologizing for the pain that it's causing you. Not because I changed my mind and I want us to get over this as if it's a mere hurdle. We will always be connected through our child, but that's all."

"Just come home with us tonight," she practically begged him.

"I will, but it's only a matter of time before I find a place."

"Of your own?" she pressed him. "Or will you stay with Jacobi?"

From the floor, they heard Suzie's little voice echo what she heard. "Cobi?"

Marti gave her husband a look, as if to say... *See! What the two of you are doing is just not right... because Jacobi's like family.*

"I'm not prepared to just pack up and go," he told her. "I guess I could get a hotel room for a week or so."

"I think you should stay with us. How about the guest room?" That idea actually appealed to him. He wouldn't share a bed with his wife, and he could still be under the same roof as his little girl. At least until he figured out his living arrangements. He wanted to stay in Cleveland to be close to the hospital and to Suzie.

He nodded. "The guest room sounds like a good idea until I have a plan."

She smiled, as if she was celebrating a tiny victory of her own. Maybe she was. Ben choosing to stay in their house would keep him from turning to Jacobi for a place to live. For now.

~

The sky was darkening, and the wind had picked up. Because there was a storm brewing, Ben and Marti agreed to meet at home and have dinner all together there. They didn't want to be stuck in a restaurant with Suzie in the middle of a thunderstorm. He said he would only be a few minutes behind them, as he had some patient files to go over at the close of the workday. He watched them walk down the hallway and get onto the elevator. When those doors met, he made his way across the hall to Jacobi's office.

Her door was closed, and he wondered if she had already left the hospital. After two taps with his knuckles, he heard her call out for him to come in.

She looked up from her desk. No smile. No greeting.

He closed the door behind him.

"Not here, Ben. I can't. Just go home to her. That's clearly what she still wants, regardless of my confession and our feelings for each other."

"I am going home," he began. "I've decided to stay in the guest room to be close to Suzie. I mean, at least until I have a long-range plan."

"You can't stay with me; not yet," she blurted out those words before she truly thought about them. *Could she really turn him away? Was protecting their reputations worth being apart? Did she even care about the truth coming out anymore?*

"Do you regret this now? Do you wish that I would have just privately chosen to stay in my marriage and try for another baby? I could have kept my feelings hid. I mean, that's what you and I have done best all this time."

"The pain we've caused Marti and knowing that Suzie will not have her daddy full-time is hard to take. We were all doing okay, surviving as we were. But being close to you again… having you touch me like only you can… makes me feel selfish and I'm suddenly doing a 180, because I want that for myself and for us. Why should either of us settle? We've got one life. I want to live it, really live it."

Ben stepped closer to her. Lightning flashed outside the window. He took both of her hands and he pulled her to her feet. A loud crack of thunder instantly followed, and then startled Jacobi. She jumped in response, and then laughed at herself, while he drew her closer to him. She was in his arms. Their lips met. Their kisses seem to have a way of beginning tenderly and escalating quickly. They shared an overwhelming passion. A desire that mounted higher and higher each time they were intimate. "We can't do this here," she spoke with her lips still on his, her tongue purposely brushing his upper lip.

"You make it very difficult for me to have any self-control," he groaned.

"We'll figure this out," she assured him. "For now, I want you to go home."

He nodded reluctantly, and eventually left her office. Jacobi sat back down on the chair behind her desk, and she thought about him. Ben Oliver was such a force in her life. Both their friendship and their working relationship was no match for anything else. She would sacrifice having more if she had to. After all, she was accustomed to always wanting more and needing more from him while having to settle for feeling lonely.

~

Unlike Ben who was driving in strong winds and a relentless downpour, Jacobi chose to wait out this storm in her office. She was in no hurry to get home. Ben, on the other hand, knew his wife and child were waiting for him and he was anxious to be out of the treacherous weather.

Only a few minutes into his drive home, Ben made a righthand turn onto Carnegie Avenue and immediately saw the backup. The rain was splashing all over his windshield, so much so that the wipers couldn't completely clear his view. He assumed, given the standstill during this horrendous rainstorm, that there was an accident scene ahead. At one point, he thought he could see red flashing lights. Having no other choice, he sat idle with the rest of the traffic. He reached for his phone on the passenger seat and sent Marti a text.

*Sitting in my car on Carnegie. Seems to be an accident that's holding up traffic in this monsoon.*

Most times, when Ben sent her a message, if he just waited a few seconds, he would see the three dots on his phone, indicating that she was typing back a reply. When he didn't see that, he placed his phone back on the seat beside him.

## Nothing Left to Give

After several minutes, traffic began to inch. And, thankfully, the rain had let up considerably. As Ben got closer, he saw multiple police cars, a fire truck, and an ambulance which appeared to be in the process of pulling away. Passerby were cruising slowly, no doubt gawking at the accident scene. Ben was no different. He saw two badly smashed up vehicles. He slammed on his brakes when he saw the backend of a white Pacifica minivan. The license plate was visible on a still intact backend, but the rest of the vehicle's front and middle resembled the likes of an accordion. Ben was at a complete stop now, stretching his body across the front seat of his car to be able to see out the passenger window. He was sure of what he read now, but he was nowhere near ready to process the shock that ricocheted throughout his body.

The personalized license plate was Oliver 3.

That was Marti's minivan.

They were the family of three.

He frantically steered his vehicle off to the shoulder. He left it running and got out and ran. Two police officers were quick to make their way over to him, just as the ambulance left the roadside, blaring its sirens.

"Wait!" Ben screamed out. "That van! It's my wife's. My family was in there." A steady rain now soaked his scrubs, his hair, and his face. But he was numb to it all.

"Let's get you back to your vehicle, safely," one of the officers pressed an open palm to Ben's chest. "The ambulance is on its way to the hospital. Do you work at Cleveland Clinic?"

Wearing scrubs, a mile and a half away from the hospital gave way to that possibility.

Ben nodded. "I'm a doctor," he struggled to catch his breath. "I need to know that my wife and little girl are going to be okay!" The excessive damage to the van was reason for alarm, but while Ben's thoughts raced and panic filled his chest, he told himself that people walked away unscathed from accidents all the time.

"You need to go back to the hospital; follow the ambulance. There was a head-on collision, and I don't know the full extent of their conditions."

"What happened out here? No," Ben regained his composure, "just tell me that they are alive." He was spitting rain from his mouth when the officer spoke again.

"Go to them. The white van crossed the center line. That's all I got. I don't want to misspeak; I was out here dealing with traffic while the paramedics did their job."

Ben turned away. He hoped with his entire being that this wasn't the police officer's way of keeping the bad news to himself so that someone else would have to share it once he returned to the hospital.

He made his way back to his car, while the same two officers stalled the traffic in both directions to allow him to safely make a U-turn toward the hospital, where he feared having to hear the fate of his family. One last look in his rearview mirror at their wrecked van, and Ben felt all his emotions tightly massed in the pit of his stomach.

# Chapter 10

It was his own stomping ground. Ben had given several years of his life to sustaining the obstetrics department at Cleveland Clinic as one of the top-ranked in the country. He wouldn't take all the credit for that, as Jacobi was by his side. He wasn't just going to sit tight in the waiting area of the ER and wait for someone to find him. When the automatic doors slid open, he rushed inside, directly to the information desk. He didn't know whether the woman in the floral smock was a nurse or a receptionist.

All he said was, "I'm Dr. Oliver, an OBGYN on the sixth floor of this hospital. I need answers about my wife and child who were in a car accident."

She made eye contact with him and then responded as she likely had all day long with frantic or impatient loved ones. "They were just brought in," she told him what he had already known, and paused, staring, as if she also wanted to say *you know the drill; sit down and wait like everyone else.*

~

Almost twenty minutes later, Ben felt a hand on his shoulder. He immediately turned to see who was there. Jacobi stared back at him with the same fear in her eyes that he felt in his own. "You heard?" he asked her.

She nodded. "Word travels fast inside these walls."

"I came across the accident as soon as I left, then I saw Marti's van..." his voice cracked. "The ambulance was just leaving the scene. No one could tell me anything about their conditions. I still don't know a damn thing!"

Jacobi leaned into him and wrapped her arms around him. He was soaking wet, but she held onto him anyway. In an instant, all their lives changed. Just minutes ago, Reeda had rushed into Jacobi's office with the awful news. Someone from the ER had been looking to notify Dr. Oliver that his wife and child were involved in a head-on collision in close proximity to the hospital. Reeda was the first to hear of the terrible news and she had been beside herself.

"Dr. Oliver?" he and Jacobi pulled away from their embrace. Ben made eye contact with a male doctor at least twenty years his senior. "If you'll come with me, I'll have some answers for you about your wife and child."

Ben looked at Jacobi. Not a word was spoken, but she knew that she was going with him.

They followed the ER doctor through the double doors. He walked only a few feet before he stopped and leaned his back against the wall in that narrow hallway. That location was as private as it was going to get for them.

# Nothing Left to Give

"They both survived the accident," he spoke those words first, as Ben and Jacobi continued to listen, to find out if there was bad news that would follow the good.

"Your little girl has several contusions and a slight concussion. She did require a few stiches on her forearm. She was incredibly lucky."

Ben sighed in relief. He needed to get to her, to hold her. He knew that she had to be terrified alone, without him or her mother. "And my wife? How is she?"

"A lot of bruising. No visible broken bones. Her face is the area of concern. We're running x-rays for possible fractures in her cheekbones, nose, and forehead. There's a sizeable, deep laceration down her left cheek, which we've closed, but have called in a plastic surgeon."

Ben swallowed hard, while Jacobi stood at his side, taking in all the same news. She could hear the relief in his voice when he spoke. "She's alive, they both survived that terrible crash. That's all that matters. We can handle the rest."

~

Still wearing her scrubs from the workday, Jacobi was walking the length of the hallway while holding Suzie in her arms. This was a distraction; walking and talking to her in a soft, soothing voice helped keep the tears at bay. There had been so much crying. She was a baby, frightened beyond words, and rightly so. It helped for her to see her daddy *and Cobi*, but she also wanted her mommy. Even though she was little, her mind had absorbed what happened in that car wreck, including seeing all the blood and knowing that her mommy was hurt. While Jacobi comforted her, Ben was able to see Marti.

He put on his bravest face as he stepped into the small cubicle in the ER that had a sliding glass door, similar to a patio door with a curtain that covered it for privacy. Ben looked closely at her, and noticed her body was very still on the gurney. There was thick gauze underneath a heavy bandage that began underneath her left eye and extended down her cheek. Her blonde curly hair was matted in blood above her forehead. He thought she was resting as he stepped closer to her, but she opened her eyes.

"They keep telling me that our baby girl is okay, but I need to see for myself." Tears pooled in her eyes. "I'm so sorry that I didn't keep her safe."

"Marti, it was an accident. Suzie has three stiches in her forearm. That's all. Otherwise, she's still perfect," he tried to smile at her. "How about you? How's your pain level?"

"I don't know. How do you measure persistent throbbing on a scale of one to ten? I'm told that I am going to need plastic surgery. I must look like a freak or something repulsive under this bandage."'

Ben shook his head. "A cut will heal. Plastic surgeons can do wonders. I don't want you to worry about that."

Marti stayed silent. It was easy for him to imply that it was just a cut; it wasn't his face. She could withstand the pain, the intense throbbing. She would endure ten times more, if she could spare having to see the imperfection on her face in the mirror. If they would ever allow her to see herself in a mirror.

"I was so scared when I saw your van at the accident scene," Ben admitted. "The weather was terrible; I've never driven in rain like that in my life. I couldn't see anything through the windshield."

"You're trying to make me blame myself less," Marti noted. "Ben, it was me. I caused that accident. I crossed the line and hit another vehicle head on. It was too late before I realized that I'd lost control."

"All that matters is you're okay, and Suzie is remarkably just fine."

"What about the people in the other car?"

"I don't know," Ben shook his head. He chided himself because he never thought to ask. He had been so worried about his own family. "I couldn't even get any information about you for the longest time."

Marti imagined what was going through his mind, if he thought she had died. At this turning point in their marriage, would it even have mattered to him? She avoided that question. "Is Suzie with the nurses? I want to see her."

Ben paused. "Jacobi was consoling her when I left to come in here. She is asking for you nonstop. She needs her mother."

"I need her, too. I'm glad she has her Cobi right now." Marti's words were genuine, and Ben knew that. He stayed quiet. In an inexplicable way, Cobi had belonged to all of them.

"I want to see them. Can you find Jacobi and have her bring Suzie in here?"

~

Ben stood back while Jacobi placed Suzie in Marti's open arms. Suzie was both perceptive and curious about her mother's face being partially bandaged. "Ouchie?"

"Yes, mommy has an ouchie, just like you do," Marti gently placed a finger on her little girl's forearm, near the stitches.

Suzie wiggled on her mommy's lap, pulling the bedsheet over her own legs too. This went on for a short while, as they all shared conversation that was awkward at times. No one was talking about the accident or the fact that Marti would likely be left with a permanent scar that she would see every time she looked at her face in the mirror. *But the ramifications of that accident could have been so much worse.*

When Suzie complained of being hungry, Ben wanted to take her down to the cafeteria. That should have been Jacobi's cue to leave, she believed, but she declined.

"I'm going stay with Marti for a while longer," she told Ben, and he tried to read the expression on her face but he couldn't. When the door closed behind them, she stood close to Marti's bedside.

"How bad does your face hurt right now?" That was a real question between friends. They held nothing back; they didn't pretend with each other.

Marti shrugged. "If it would just stop throbbing. Maybe if I knew what it looked like, I could relax."

"You haven't seen it?"

"They advised against it. All I know is that the laceration was sutured because it was too deep to be glued, which would have prevented further scaring."

"I can help you take a look," Jacobi offered.

"Aren't you qualified for the other end?" Marti quipped.

Jacobi smirked. "I think I can handle peeling back a bandage and helping you to get a better idea of what you're dealing with." Jacobi bent over the chair behind her and searched through her handbag to locate her makeup compact that had a mirror underneath the lid.

She placed that compact on top the sheet that covered Marti's lap, and then she carefully peeled back the tape that bordered the bandage on her left cheek. When she lifted the gauze pad, Jacobi saw how the laceration formed an uneven line from beneath her eye and down to the corner of her mouth. The size and the severity of that cut alarmed Jacobi, but she didn't let her emotion show. Before she had the chance to forewarn Marti to take it slow, to go easy on herself, she had already lifted the small mirror closer to her face.

There were instant tears in her eyes "Well, fuck," she muttered. "It looks as awful as it feels."

Jacobi didn't hesitate to reach for her hand, to comfort her. It was almost as if it didn't matter that she crossed the line with Ben; somehow the two of them still shared a special friendship.

Marti didn't hate her or want to force her out of her sight. While that still confused Jacobi, she didn't want to question it.

"Right now, it's fresh and raw, so it's going to look and feel the worst. Time to heal will change that."

"True. But, do you want to know something else? Plastic surgeons aren't magicians. This will never fully disappear," she pointed to her face. "So now I'm even more imperfect to your perfect."

"What?" Marti's words caught Jacobi off guard.

"You," Marti put her on the spot. "I'll never be you. Taller, thinner, strikingly beautiful — and flawless compared to me, especially now. It's no wonder Ben wants you."

"No one is without flaws, and no one should ever want to be anyone else besides themselves." Jacobi didn't react to her direct comment about Ben.

"I want to be the woman that my husband wants." There it was again. Now that Marti knew the truth, Ben would always be the man that remained between them. They never ceased eye contact with each other. Their honesty was suddenly uncomfortably raw.

"None of us can change how we feel," Jacobi tried to defend all of them. And she wondered if there would ever be a way for them to get through this. Somehow.

"So that's your excuse? You've always been in love with Ben, but now you're once and for all done hiding it. What about us? Our friendship? What about Suzie? She adores you. I don't think she will understand that Auntie Cobi is now sharing a bed

# Nothing Left to Give

with her daddy. It's sickening, you know, what the two of you are doing! You're wrecking a family. You're breaking us apart, piece by piece, just to have something that neither of you tried half as hard to get when you had the chance. It makes no damn sense to me."

"I wish things were different," Jacobi spoke the truth.

"Which means nothing, right? We're back to you winning and me at a loss for what to do with the rest of my life."

"You have a child to think about."

"I have thought about her. Over and over, I have this haunting image in my mind of you and Ben becoming a family with my daughter... and with babies of your own. I can't and I won't watch that happen. I will not let it."

Jacobi saw something shift in Marti's demeanor. Her eyes were suddenly cold and heartless. She understood the disappointment and anger, but this was something more. *Different*.

"I crossed the line on purpose."

"What are you talking about?" Jacobi pressed her. "What line?"

"The car accident wasn't really... an accident. Now do you understand when I say that I will not sit back and allow you to take my family?"

# Chapter 11

The timing could not have been worse when Ben returned with Suzie, carrying a to-go container of macaroni and cheese for her to eat in Marti's cubicle. Jacobi stepped back from Marti's bed, but she could not take her eyes off her.

*She purposely endangered her own life and the life of her child. What had been her initial plan? Suicide plus one?*

It stunned Jacobi to know that Marti's mental health was spiraling. Ben's decision to leave her had left her feeling unstable and desperate. At this point, Jacobi wanted to press Marti for more, but she was afraid to make a move. Oddly, Marti trusted Jacobi with her shocking admission but there was no way in hell that this was something she could keep quiet. Ben had to know. Suzie sadly needed protection from her own mother. And Marti was certifiable for immediate psychiatric help.

Jacobi's mind continued to reel while the nurses came in and out of Marti's temporary home in the ER. She was told that the plastic surgeon would see her tomorrow, so overnight she would be admitted to a patient room.

"What do you want me to do with Suzie? I can take her home tonight, or I could have Jacobi help us out, if you want me to stay here with you?" Ben glanced from his wife to Jacobi while he spoke. He had no idea what had just transpired between them.

"You should go home," Marti told him, and she looked directly at Jacobi.

"I can stay for a while," Jacobi spoke, believing that's what Marti ultimately wanted, and she wanted answers for herself.

"Are you sure?" Ben questioned how the two of them could stand to be in the same room with each other. It was as if their friendship had not been affected at all by the affair and his decision to leave their marriage.

"I think that's a good idea," Marti noted, and Jacobi couldn't help but wonder if she was on an obvious mission to keep Ben and her apart, and to prevent Jacobi from telling him or anyone else the truth about the accident. But what was her end game? That was something Jacobi feared right now, especially because she knew it had to involve her. After all, why had Marti confessed only to her?

Ben and Suzie said their goodbyes, and Marti promised to call him through the night if anything changed. For now, they both knew that meeting with a plastic surgeon was the next immediate step.

The moment the door was sealed, Jacobi spoke.

"What is going on?" The feigned innocent expression on Marti's face nearly sent Jacobi reeling. "Why did you tell me that you tried to kill yourself and Suzie?" It felt even more devastating to hear herself say those words aloud. "Please retract that as bullshit, like you were talking out of your head or something from your injuries in the accident."

Marti folded her hands on her lap as she sat still and upright on that gurney. Her face was partially obscured with a bandage, but Jacobi could detect an odd serenity in her eyes. She didn't look like someone who was rattled from a car accident, or distraught from a failed suicide. *Was that what the accident was?* Jacobi had unanswered questions. *Had Marti's intention really been to risk her life and her child's life, all for some sort of twisted plan to keep her husband?*

"I told you because you are the only one who can help me by halting Ben's plans to start over with his life — with you this time."

"Are you threatening me?" Jacobi was not afraid to call her out; she wasn't that damn fragile. "Are you bargaining with Suzie's life? If Ben and I aren't together, then she will be safe? Is that what you are trying to do here?"

"You've always been very perceptive," was all Marti offered in response to Jacobi's accusations.

"I don't even know who you are anymore!" Jacobi spat at her. She was visibly shaken; her hands were trembling. "You need help, or there will be extreme measures taken so that you never see Suzie again." Jacobi backed up, making her way to the door so she could escape that madness.

"No one else is going to know about this," Marti reacted. And again, she was strangely calm. "You're not going to run to Ben in some sort of heroic effort to save the day. I'll deny it, I'll blame the car accident; I hit my head and I'm confused. That's not unheard of."

"I can't be near you right now," Jacobi grabbed the door handle and aggressively slid the glass sideways in a rush, as she left without turning around to close it or to respond to Marti calling her name.

~

Jacobi showed up at Ben's house after he had tucked Suzie into bed. He explained that the stitches in her arm had not seemed to bother her at all, but he did intend to wake her up every hour through the night, just as a precaution from the mild concussion. Jacobi mostly stayed quiet, allowing him to speak, while she tried to piece together the words in her mind that she needed to say to him.

"I'm glad you stopped by," he said to her as the two of them stood in the kitchen. Ben offered her something to drink, but Jacobi declined.

"I came straight from the hospital," she tugged at the scrubs she had been wearing all day.

"How did Marti seem to you? I'm still surprised by how close she still wants to be with you, considering… I mean, why isn't she angry?"

"I had the same thoughts, at first," Jacobi began, "but I've since realized that Marti does not want to let go. The thought of losing you, and the family that she has with you and Suzie, is too much for her. She's out of her mind."

Ben creased his brow. "What? Don't you think that's kind of extreme? I mean, just because she's trying to hold onto everything doesn't mean she's losing it."

Jacobi sighed. This was harder to tell him than she realized it would be. "Marti may have some mental health issues like her mother did," she was careful to phrase her words in a way that she didn't have to say she was suicidal. Not yet. That was going to be a shock for Ben to absorb, as it was still unbelievable to Jacobi.

"Her mother? No. Marti would never."

"Take her own life?" Jacobi interjected. "All we know about her mother was what Marti told us; she was fine until her husband left her. And then she killed herself."

"Why are you comparing Marti to her? We both know how much pain her mother's suicide caused her. She would never do that to Suzie."

"Apparently you're right about that… that's why she tried to take Suzie with her."

Ben looked confused. "You're not making any sense."

"I didn't want to believe it either, but Marti told me that she steered her van over the line to hit that other vehicle head-on, on purpose."

Ben profusely shook his head. He pushed off the counter that he had been leaning his lower back against. "She said those exact words to you? Why? There must be an explanation for that craziness. I mean, the ER doctor clearly missed something. Marti is talking out of her head which means she could have a brain injury!"

"That's certainly possible," Jacobi spoke gently to him. "But, she was very clear when she spoke to me in no uncertain terms. She said that she will not sit back and watch me take her family. She can't handle the thought of us... together... with Suzie... and possibly with children of our own someday. Those were her words! She said I am the only one who can stop her desperate measures, if I end my relationship with you."

"Marti and Suzie were in a terrible accident today. An accident!" Ben emphasized. "That rainstorm was the absolute worst. No one could see anything on that road. Marti needs another CT scan. That's what's going on here." Ben reached into his pocket for his cell phone. She stood quietly while he called the ER at Cleveland Clinic. She listened while he spoke to one of the nurses, and word for word, he instructed her to have the doctor run more tests, namely a CT scan as soon as possible. Ben spoke as if he was the one in charge. And when he ended the call, he was certain that he was about to get answers that would explain Marti's behavior.

He saw Jacobi staring at him when he ended the call. "Why are you doubting this?" he all but snapped at her.

"I know you're hurting; you almost lost them both today. But if she did it on purpose, there's no time to waste refusing to accept that. You have to deal with it now. Marti needs help, and Suzie needs protection from her own mother."

"That's not true, and it's certainly unfair to Marti. She was seriously hurt in that crash, and she felt awful for putting Suzie in any danger."

"I know what she said to me, Ben. She's shoving an ultimatum at me, and she's using her own child in the process!"

Ben heard her out. He listened, but every word that Jacobi was trying so desperately to get him to absorb went unheard, because he believed there was a medical explanation for Marti to speak out of her head. Jacobi could see the hurt and disappointment in his eyes, but it was displaced. Instead of feeling pained and alarmed by his wife's dire actions, those emotions were directed at Jacobi.

He didn't believe her.

# Chapter 12

Jacobi went home and showered. She was on call tonight for both her patients and Ben's, since he needed the night off to be with Suzie. She never asked him what he was going to do about seeing patients in the morning. The only thing they talked about was Marti, and they continued to disagree to the point of arguing about her state of mind. Finally, Jacobi left his house and he never stopped her.

It was an uneventful night, so Jacobi had not returned to her office at the hospital until morning. She barely had a chance to settle in before Reeda was standing right behind her while she put her lunch in the refrigerator in the break room.

"Any news about Dr. Oliver's wife?"

"Nothing more than what I knew last night," Jacobi told her. "She's supposed to see a plastic surgeon this morning, so depending on how soon she's able to have surgery, she could be discharged to go home." That thought scared Jacobi. Would Ben really trust leaving her alone with Suzie?

"That accident could have been much worse, but how terrible for her to have facial scarring. She's such a pretty little thing."

"I wish none of it happened for all their sakes," Jacobi spoke on behalf of herself as well. *She wished that nothing had happened. Period.* If she had not given into Ben and her undying desires for him, Marti would be fine and Suzie would still be safe.

"Life's unexpected comes in eye opening ways sometimes," Reeda commented, as if she knew something more, but Jacobi realized that was not possible. She was just a wise, mature woman who had lived through her share of ups and downs.

"I agree," was all Jacobi responded as she left the room.

Three floors below, Ben was walking into Marti's room. He had taken a call after midnight from the ER doctor. Another CT scan had shown the same results that were previously documented following the car accident. There was no serious head trauma. A mild concussion, at best, the doctor informed him. Ben never questioned his ability to treat a patient, but he did ask him if it was common for a patient to talk out of their head following trauma.

Ben ended that call believing the sheer shock from the accident, or quite possibly the pain medication, was what triggered Marti to act out of character and lie to Jacobi. It still unnerved him that Jacobi believed Suzie could actually be in real danger from her own mother.

Marti was sitting up on the hospital bed with a breakfast tray on her lap. "Looks like you have an appetite," Ben said to

## Nothing Left to Give

her when he stepped inside her room.

"Really? You try to eat when one side of your face is bandaged and hurting like a son of a bitch every time you attempt to chew."

He grimaced. "I'm sorry that happened to you. If I could have protected you and Suzie, I would have. You know that." He had since wished they would have all left the hospital together and followed each other home. Instead, he stayed so he could be with Jacobi. There was some nagging guilt there that wouldn't subside for him.

"I know," she tried to smile at him. "How's Sooz feeling? I thought about her all night." Ben noted that those were not the words or the caring nature of a woman who wanted to hurt her own child. Earlier, he had texted her about leaving Suzie with their neighbor, Dana, today. He wanted to make sure that she agreed because they were the kind of parents who didn't just leave their child with anyone.

"She's as good as new, really. She'll be fine. Just concentrate on healing so you can go home to her. She misses you."

Marti wished he would have implied that she would be going home to both of them, not just Suzie. "I miss her, too. I want us all to be together, Ben. Has any of this changed your mind? I mean, my God, we could have both died in that accident."

Ben creased his brow. "What do you mean by that?"

"You could have lost us. We're your family, Ben."

"I was beside myself with worry. I couldn't bear it if something really bad happened to either of you."

Marti smiled. He did still care about her.

"I've opted to have the plastic surgery on my face tomorrow, as soon as possible, so I can get back to my life, our life, together, Ben. I'm going to need your support."

"I understand," he said, knowing that it would not be easy for Marti to deal with having a visible imperfection on her face. That would be difficult for anyone. "I'm not leaving, Marti. I'll be living in our home, at least until you are fully recovered."

"I'm going to change your mind," she spoke confidently. "You will see that it's me who you want to spend your life with. There was a time when you believed that, so I know it's possible for you to get back to that mindset. We have a daughter to raise together, as a unit, a solid family. Ben, you saw firsthand how quickly something can happen. Suzie could have died."

He studied her face for a moment. A mother's greatest fear was supposed to be losing her child, yet Marti had so nonchalantly spoken those words. Twice now.

"I want you to focus on yourself and getting well," he spoke, choosing not to address her eagerness to reconcile. Or, how she freely used their child to get to him, to stay connected to him. That had not gone unnoticed to Ben.

"Promise me that you will help me," she reached out her hand to him.

He stepped closer and held her hand. "I will. You can count on me to always be there for you, Marti."

Even knowing her face would be forever scarred from an accident that she caused, Marti had a sense of renewed hope. The risk that she took with both her life and Suzie's was worth it to her to have her husband back.

~

Hours after she saw her patients and squeezed in as many as she could from Ben's schedule, Jacobi was tired, but she wasn't going home until she made her way a few floors down to Marti's room. She knew that she was having plastic surgery tomorrow. Word got around quickly in that hospital. Having to hear it through the grapevine bothered her though. Ben could have let her know. He hadn't reached out to her at all.

Her office door was closed when she heard someone walking down the hall. She got up from her desk chair and peeked outside her door just as Ben's door was closing. "Hey!" she used her voice to stop him from completely shutting it. No one else was around, so she spoke her mind. "Is this how we're acting now?" Her implication was direct and spiteful. "No communication and hiding behind closed doors from each other?"

Ben looked at her as she crossed the hallway and now stood inside the frame of his doorway. "Tell me how you really feel," he gave her a soft smile, and she pushed her way inside his office and closed the door behind her.

"You know how I really feel, and that's the problem. We've made such a mess of everything." She sat on the edge of his desk, and he walked over to her.

"When I came across that accident and saw Marti's van, I was so panicked. I kept saying, that's my family in there. My wife. My child. Their lives were spared, but I can't shake the guilt. Part of me feels like this was somehow my fault."

"You want to stay with them," were the only words that Jacobi could bring herself to say.

"I think after all that's happened, that's what I should want."

"You're confusing me."

"How confused do you think I feel? Marti is counting on me to see her through this."

"Right," Jacobi agreed. "But I do wonder what she was counting on when she purposely put herself and Suzie in serious danger."

Ben visibly sighed. "I don't want to believe that's true."

"Did you ask her?"

"No. She's fragile right now; she's about to have reconstructive surgery on her face, not knowing what that lasting scar will turn out to look like after the plastic surgeon says that's the best he can do."

"I wouldn't wish that on anyone," Jacobi's words were sincere, "but I felt a lot less sympathy for her the moment she admitted to crossing the line and purposely causing that crash!"

"The ER doctor ran a second CT scan, which didn't show anything more than the first one. If Marti suffered from a concussion, it was mild."

"Your theory was wrong then."

"I need you to talk to her again. I want to put my ear up to the damn door and actually hear those words from her mouth," Ben was insistent.

"What you're saying then is my word isn't enough for you?"

Ben stepped closer to her. The sincerity in his eyes begged her to pay attention to him. "What I need you to understand is she's my wife, the mother of my child. I will always care about her. But if I she tried to end my little girl's life, I will be done with her forever. I will have her committed and take Suzie away from her. Don't you see? I can't act until I know for sure… before I let myself believe something so awful to be the truth."

# Chapter 13

Jacobi was completely focused. She took note when the thirty-something mother, now trusting her to deliver her second baby, said her pain was an 8 out of 10 on the pain scale because her contractions were so strong and fast, with very little relief between them.

"Just hold on a few more minutes, an epidural is coming," Jacobi reassured her.

Not more than a minute later, the woman begged for that epidural. Reeda was also in the labor and delivery room, and she quickly answered her.

"We paged the anesthesiologist," Reeda's loud voice carried across the room, yet it still had a calm and soothing effect on everyone. "He is on his way."

Another contraction came and went. Jacobi was near, watching her patient as she slumped back down on the bed, breathing a heavy sigh and placing her hands on the giant round belly protruding from her body. Just as Jacobi was about to tell her to expect three minutes of peace until the contractions would come again, the woman folded her body forward and screamed in agony.

Jacobi lunged toward her, as she immediately recognized the signs of what happened when her patient cried out how she felt as if her stomach had exploded. Her whole body then began to convulse.

The next 10 minutes were crucial. Jacobi's patient was in extreme pain, to the extent that she couldn't breathe. Within seconds, Jacobi had sprung into action.

"I can't find the baby's heartbeat. Get the anesthesiologist in here — she needs an epidural! Look at her vital signs. Get an oxygen mask on her now!"

Seven nurses were now with Jacobi as they thrusted the gurney into the operating room. The anesthesiologist gave the spinal anesthetic to numb her lower body, and within two minutes, Dr. Jacobi pulled a limp blue baby out of a broken uterus. The baby had a low heart rate, which was a bad sign, and no breathing effort, which was a very bad sign. The entire OR was working to save the baby's life. In that sterile room with bright lights and surgical instruments that were used to save lives, he was immediately intubated and rushed off to the neonatal intensive care unit. Jacobi had been watching them work on the baby from afar, and she overheard their words.

There was panic and there were tears in that OR in the aftermath.

"What happened to me? Is my baby alive?"

Jacobi needed to prep to stitch her patient's pelvis. Her uterus had ruptured from the pressure of the labor. It tore through the incision from a previous C-section.

"Your uterus tore and the baby slipped into your abdomen," Jacobi stitched as she explained what happened. "This condition normally causes a momma to lose a lot of blood, which can lead to organ failure. You were incredibly fortunate that the baby didn't tear any of your uterine blood vessels when he bursted out of your uterus."

"I need to know something about my baby!" she cried.

"All I know is when they intubated him, he fought the endotracheal tube, which was a good sign and I heard someone say that his color was beginning to return." Jacobi paused and looked behind her, clear across the room. "Reeda? Can you get us an update on the baby?" As Jacobi finished her last stitch, Reeda hurried out of the room.

Jacobi never left the OR; she stayed with her patient who was a single mother and initially planned to deliver her baby alone. That fact had touched Jacobi more than she realized it would when everything had gone wrong. This woman needed someone by her side if Reeda returned with awful news.

That wasn't the case though, because when the OR door swung open, Reeda had a spring in her step and a wide smile on her face. "Dr. Jacobi, I have good news."

Jacobi silently sighed in relief. "I'd like you to tell the baby's momma exactly what you found out in NICU."

Reeda winked at her and then delivered the best news. The baby boy was going to be fine. He was already extubated, which was said to be a great sign. Although he still needed some extra oxygen to breathe, the NICU nurses were already calling him a little fighter.

~

Jacobi made her way into the locker room. She was coming down from the adrenaline rush of being in labor and delivery, and then having to abruptly rush to the operating room following a life-threatening complication. She thrived in that hospital setting, but sometimes she needed to recheck her emotions. Babies that didn't survive was a lot to absorb as the acting physician in charge. It took her days to recover from a loss when it tragically did happen. She was grateful that both her patient's life and the baby's had been spared today. There was enough weighing on Jacobi's heart right now, which made her think of Ben. Uterine ruptures were rare, so this was definitely a case that she would discuss with him, as doctors and as confidants. But he was on another floor in that hospital now, waiting for Marti's surgery to be over.

Jacobi sat back on the sofa, tucked along a far wall in the locker room. Just as she began to breathe steadily again, the door swung open. When she saw Reeda, she expected to be summoned for another patient who needed her. Sometimes deliveries came in pairs, or even threes. She at least hoped for the next one to be less eventful. Just a typical baby-meets-world.

She started to move to her feet, but Reeda stopped her. "Sit back, honey. I'm only checking on you. That was some excitement, huh?"

"Honestly? That was my first real-life uterine rupture." She wasn't talking about the times she studied it in medical school or heard about it through a testimonial.

"Dr. Jacobi, you truly are something else. Never ceasing to amaze me in all the years of watching you work. You're the likes of a child prodigy."

Jacobi laughed. "You're forgetting I'm 35 years old."

"But I've got decades on you," Reeda cackled. "Just accept the well-deserved compliment."

"Okay. Thank you for repeatedly lifting me up even when I think I can't possibly go any higher from your perspective."

"For you, there's always higher. A success like you knows no limits," she praised her. "I imagine you're anxious to fill in Dr. Oliver or to compare notes as you two often do."

Jacobi inevitably lost her smile. "I am, but as we all know, he has other things taking up space in his mind right now."

"Have you heard how the surgery is going?"

"No, and a part of me wants to take the elevator down there and sit beside him in that waiting room." Jacobi was quick to stop talking. She was always careful not to give herself away.

Reeda studied her for a long moment. The iris of her eyes coincided with her dark skin, which made the whites of her eyes prominent. "I watched you two many moons ago, it seems, as interns. I saw the sparks fly from day one. Anyone with eyes couldn't overlook that. Many would have described it as two young and eager medical minds connecting how only those types can. You know, those stereotypical brilliant minds that are on the cusp of saving the world, one patient at a time." Jacobi halfheartedly rolled her eyes, as Reeda continued talking. "I saw something else, though; something between the two of you that I wondered if it would make or break the dynamics, if you know what I mean."

"I don't think I want to know," Jacobi quipped.

"But you do know."

"I don't appreciate the insinuation," Jacobi used her doctor tone with her.

"Maybe you just don't want to hear it. Hard truths are the toughest ones to face. Those are the things we think no one else can see simply because we won't let them."

Jacobi didn't have a response. Perhaps she wanted to adapt the old adage of not saying anything at all if she didn't have a nice comeback.

"It's not my business," Reeda began again.

"Then let's keep it that way," Jacobi certainly wished she would.

"It's as if you and Dr. Oliver have invented your own language. You've built it, here, inside these hospital walls. It's a language that neither of you will likely ever speak with anyone else. Don't confuse that with something more. It's a shared passion for the trade. That's really all it can be, right? I mean, his wife and child need him. Now more than ever, I would say."

"If I don't react to what you're implying, will that be perceived as guilt?" Jacobi questioned her. "Because, right now, I don't feel like defending myself or my relationship with Ben on any level."

"You don't have to defend or explain," Reeda stated. "I've witnessed how you have focused on yourself and your goals while you've watched him figure out his feelings and what he wants from life. It's time for you to realize this false obligation that you have to be waiting in the wings."

Jacobi gave this wise, perceptive, but sometimes intrusive woman full-on eye contact, but she never spoke a word. She was afraid to. This was between her and Ben. And, for now, that's where it would stay.

# Chapter 14

She didn't stay away. When her shift ended, Jacobi went to him. He was alone in the waiting room doing what people do when the time filled with anxiety drags on. Momentarily, Ben wasn't pacing the floors, which Jacobi would bet he had already done. Right now, he was leaning back on a chair in the corner with his arms folded across his chest. He saw her the moment she stepped into the room.

His wavy hair looked disheveled in the way it did when he ran his fingers through it if he was tired or overthinking.

Jacobi sat on the chair beside him. "Any word on how it's going in there?"

"Well," Ben answered. "They've checked in with me a few times. She should be in recovery soon." The surgery had been expected to take three hours, but after a late start, he had now been waiting for almost five hours.

"How's Suzie?"

"Having a fun time with the neighbor kids," he smiled. "She's the littlest one, so Dana told me they are doting on her, carrying her around like a baby doll."

Jacobi smiled. "She *is* a little doll." It was incomprehensible to her that Marti would purposely bring harm to her.

It was as if Ben could read her mind. "Everything feels so uncertain." He wanted to reach for her, but of course he refrained because anyone could walk in and see them. "I was so ready to move on with our lives. I mean, I knew it wouldn't be an easy adjustment for Suzie and clearly for Marti as well, but how did everything go so wrong?"

Jacobi gave him a look that was borderline frustration, as if to say that he knew exactly how. It was Marti's fault. "Where do you plan to go from here, Ben?" She damn well wanted to know. It was odd to her how she had lived her life alongside him and his family for so many years, but now things felt drastically different.

"I need to give Marti time to heal… but I want to know the truth about the accident," he told her. Jacobi agreed, but stayed silent. Honestly, she didn't even know what to say anymore. "I wonder if we will ever look back at this time in our lives and say that we made it. Not unscathed. But that we survived."

"I hope so," she replied, just as a surgical nurse entered the waiting room and interrupted them. Marti was in recovery, awake, and asking for her husband.

Ben stood up. He was going to go to her. Jacobi, however, wanted to avoid her. Everything about their last conversation scared the hell out of her.

As the nurse was waiting to escort Ben to the recovery room, he turned to Jacobi. "Are you coming?"

She felt as if he had put her on the spot, but Jacobi was never one to shy away from speaking her mind. *No. You just go. Fill me in later.* Those were all the things she could have said to him. Instead, as oddly as it seemed, they were all in this together.

~

Marti was awake when they entered the cubicle, another temporary room for her, a place they called recovery where she would be watched closely following surgery and before she was moved into a patient room of her own. Jacobi couldn't help but wonder what things would be like when she was discharged from the hospital and sent home.

"Hey there…" Ben spoke quietly as Jacobi stood beside him.

"Hi," she responded in a raspy voice, while she focused on them standing there together. Her face was thickly bandaged to cover the laceration that the plastic surgeon was miraculously supposed to make look better. Still, there would always be some type of scarring there as a constant reminder.

"How are you feeling?" Jacobi felt pressured to say something, and that was just the next obvious question.

"Groggy, but okay," she answered Jacobi, and then made eye contact with Ben. "How's our princess doing?"

"Very well. Dana and her crew are spoiling her," Ben smiled, genuinely, because anytime that he spoke of his little girl, all was right with the world.

"I want to go home to her." The sentiment was nice, but Jacobi was so closed off to feeling anything but repulsed toward Marti that she ignored her. Ben, however, did not.

"Soon enough," he tried to sound encouraging. "At most, you'll be here one or two more nights."

"Then what?" Marti's voice suddenly sounded less weak.

"You'll go home," Ben stated as a matter of fact, just as one of the recovery nurses stepped into that cubicle to check Marti's vitals.

"With you? And our daughter?" Marti pressed him even though they no longer had as much privacy as a cubicle offered.

Ben nodded. Jacobi fidgeted from one foot to the other.

"I'm Kristen, your recovery nurse, and it looks like you are ready to be moved to a room of your own." Her voice was chipper despite the obvious tension inside that small space.

"Hi Kristen," Marti tried to smile with a partially obscured face. "This is my husband, Ben. He's an OBGYN here in this hospital. Oh, and that's Jacobi, his colleague and the woman who's screwing him."

## Nothing Left to Give

The nurse's eyes widened, Ben clenched his jaw, and Jacobi turned around to walk out. She wouldn't cause a scene. Marti had already made a fool of them on her own.

"I'll just step out for a moment," the wide-eyed nurse uttered under her breath. Clearly, she needed to escape and no one stopped her. Marti, however, did prevent Jacobi from leaving.

"Wait."

Jacobi turned sideways as if her body language was supposed to communicate that she was still halfway out the door and Marti's call back had better be worth her effort to stay. Ben looked from one woman to the other and then spun his head back to Marti. "I don't know if you are still coming off the anesthesia, or—"

"Don't make excuses for her," Jacobi snapped, as she tried to make a real attempt to keep her voice low. Behind her bandage, Marti smirked at the potential spat between them.

Ben shook his head, probably at the situation itself. It was a damn mess between the three of them, and he inevitably was the one most at fault.

"I'm sorry," Marti attempted to explain herself. "I have no filter right now. Seriously, my head feels disconnected."

Jacobi rolled her eyes. Ben didn't react.

"I'll blame the drugs when the nurse comes back in," Marti suggested, and Ben stopped her.

"Just don't, okay? Leave it. Jacobi stopped by the waiting room after her shift to see how your surgery went. That's all. She cares, okay?"

"Of course," Marti looked in Jacobi's direction and for a moment it seemed as if nothing had changed between them.

And that was the strangest part of all this. One moment Marti was completely fine, and the next she was vengeful and possibly on the brink of saying, or doing, things that she could not control.

# Chapter 15

Three days later, Marti came home. Her large bandage with soft gauze underneath was gone and in place of it was a smaller, narrow one. Each time that she removed what covered the scar on her face, she became a little more used to what she saw. She was anticipating when it would be fully healed, to be able to apply makeup to conceal it.

Ben and Jacobi were seeing less and less of each other, as he was by his wife's side most of the time. His return to work was planned for next week. While Jacobi was swamped juggling some of his patients with all of hers, she preferred the distance between them. It was just easier that way, as the future they so briefly thought was going to happen for the two of them was now looking bleak. For the time being, anyway, Ben's place was with his family. Jacobi kept her relief from that to herself, but she felt it in spades. As long as Ben was around all the time, Suzie would be safe. Jacobi hadn't forgotten Marti's threat.

At the end of another workday, Jacobi checked the messages on her phone. Three texts were from Ben.

*She's home and doing well.*

*Sincerely happy to be reunited with Suzie.* There was a picture attached of the two of them playing on the living room floor.

*Marti wants to see you.*

Jacobi had mixed emotions as she read each one of those messages. Her strongest feelings, however, pertained to Marti summoning her in some weird way. She didn't respond to any of Ben's messages. She just went home to be alone, hoping that the evening would fade so she could go to bed and get up and do her job all over again. It was the only thing that kept her mind preoccupied.

She turned her phone off to avoid knowing if Ben tried to reach her. It was after eight o'clock when she wanted to turn off her mind from the replay of worry she had for Suzie and the frustration that was building toward Ben. He needed to open his eyes about Marti. And what bothered her more than that was his promises to her suddenly made her feel like nothing more than the other woman.

She laid on her bed, covered up to her chin, staring up at the ceiling. Her eyes had adjusted to the dark room. She wished for sleep. Restful sleep. It had been days since she had been able to fully relax. She turned her body, raised her head and fluffed her pillow, just as she heard knocking on her front door. She wasn't startled. She just had half a mind not to let him in.

Instead, she got out of bed and shoved her arms into the terrycloth robe that was draped over the armchair near the nightstand beside her bed. She made her way through her condo, turned on a lamp in the living room, and then stood close to the opposite side of the locked door. That's when Ben reassured her that it was him.

"Hey, it's me. Please open the door."

She turned the deadbolt, cracked the door just enough so that he could see her, and then she allowed him to push it open wider and step inside.

"Were you in bed?"

"It's my only avoidance mechanism these days. If I force sleep, I don't have to think about everything that's gone wrong with my life."

"Our life."

She shrugged. "You can't seem to make that work."

"That's unfair. You know as soon as Marti recovers—"

"It's more than waiting for a wound to heal. She's mentally ill, Ben. Whether you believe that or not, it isn't something that I want to disagree about anymore. And right now you are being careless leaving her alone with Suzie."

"She's not alone. Dana stopped by, so I used the excuse that I needed to catch up on paperwork at the hospital."

"I'm sure Marti was onto you."

"I don't care." He tried to reach for her, but she backed away.

"So now you want to have an affair?" she asked him. "We could have done that to begin with, never needing to tell Marti the truth. Instead, you made broken promises that I fell for."

"None of that is true and you know it. All I want is for us to move on with our lives together. And I don't care how angry you act or how adamantly you deny it, I know you want the same."

She attempted to look away until he placed his open palm on her cheek. She looked at him, directly into his eyes. "I need to stop," she paused to think about what she had to say. "I have to stop making what I feel like are permanent decisions based on temporary emotions."

"Temporary emotions?" he questioned her judgement. "Nothing that we've felt for each other has ever been short-lived."

"I need some space. I can't get so wrapped up in you and the idea of us actually being together. If it's going to happen, God knows I'll let it. But if it's just our wishful fantasy, then I need to prepare myself."

"I have three things to say to you and you better listen good," he spoke with a little mischief in his eyes, and she tried not to fall a little harder for him. "I love you. I need you in my life all the time. And, I promise that you and I are going to get our chance."

"Mere words," she halfheartedly teased him.

"Ah, I see how you want to be. Do actions suit you better, Reese Jacobi?"

"It's just Jacobi," she seriously reminded him, as he undid the loose knot on her robe at her waist. He opened it, looking at her standing there in only a t-shirt with likely nothing but a pair of panties underneath. He surely wanted to find out.

"Let me show you how much you mean to me." He really wasn't asking her for permission, and he essentially didn't need it as his lips softly met hers and she never fought to respond to him.

He pressed his body into hers and kissed her long and full on the mouth. Giving in completely to what they both wanted now, and have always wanted, she led him by the hand to her bedroom. Standing at the foot-end of her bed, he lifted the loose-fitting t-shirt over her head. Her breasts were bare, and her pink panties were dainty. He cupped her chest with both of his hands. He thumbed her nipples until she arched her back for him as he slightly bent his knees to put his mouth where his hands had been. He encouraged her to keep standing as he braced her lower back as he made his way down her body. He knelt before her and slipped off those pretty panties. He parted her legs, gripping her thighs and kissing her core. He caressed the most sensitive part of her body, attentive to her reactions — every moan, and the way that her body relaxed for him and then simultaneously tightened with arousal. His fingers were inside her and his mouth was on her down there. And she had never had a more explosive reaction for anyone else. She gripped his shoulders with her release, and she called out the name of the man who possessed her heart. He guided her down on the bed, and when he entered her, slowly and fully, neither one of them wanted the moment to end. The intensity of their passion, their connection, and the depth of their love was something they could no longer deny.

# Chapter 16

The following morning, Jacobi was backing her car out of the garage and down the driveway when she saw a woman walking on the sidewalk at the edge of her yard. She would know that walk anywhere. Jacobi's mother lived almost four miles away from her condo, and her walk route always led her right by there. Likely, on purpose. She and her mother were on good terms, but they weren't close confidants. It's just the way they had always been. They lived separate lives, and sometimes Jacobi would admit to herself in frustration that she just didn't have the energy for Shauna.

She shifted her car into park, swung open the door, and got out. In her navy scrubs, sans a layer, Jacobi realized she should have worn a light jacket this morning. Her mother was waving as she climbed the slightly inclined driveway. "Good morning, Reese. I'd say it's perfect timing on my part to finally get to see you. My goodness, how long has it been? I know you're an important doctor and all but, for chrissakes, I could die and then decompose before you'd ever notice."

Jacobi refrained from rolling her eyes. "Hopefully the stench would get your neighbor's attention sooner than later."

## Nothing Left to Give

"Not funny, Shauna reacted, as Jacobi recognized again how they shared a few similar features. Long legs. Dark hair. High cheekbones. "So what's been going on in your life?" Those details would be the very last thing that Jacobi would ever want to reveal to her mother. *She was having an affair with Ben... and his wife was consequently losing her mind over it.*

"Not much else other than working, eating, and sleeping."

"Well that's boring," Shauna didn't hide her disappointment. "You're too young to live like that already."

"Yet you always tell me that 35 years old is getting up there and I should make a life for myself before my eggs are all shriveled up and useless to me."

Her mother nodded repeatedly. "So it seems that you do listen to me..."

"I should let you get back on the trail so I'm not late for work," Jacobi not so subtly tried to move her along.

"In a second. I've been meaning to tell you that there's a new face on those hospital grounds since just a few weeks ago, but he's a familiar one to you."

These were the types of silly games that her mother liked to play. Wouldn't it have been better to just come right out and say who she was speaking of? She always used a dramatic lead-in before she shared any type of information. "I have no idea who might be newly employed at Cleveland Clinic."

"He's not new to you," Shauna giggled out loud like a schoolgirl with a secret.

"Right. Who?" Jacobi's tone was as if to say, she really didn't care to know.

"Matthew Huegen. He's into sports medicine and just moved back here for a job at Cleveland Clinic."

Matthew Huegen was a high school classmate of Jacobi's. She met him during her freshman year. He was her first crush, and also her first kiss. But that was the extent of it. They never dated; they never had sex. Yet her mother always called that boy the one that got away from Jacobi.

"I had no idea," was Jacobi's only response.

"Well you may wanna look him up and purposely fall into his path!" Shauna spoke as if that was the best idea ever.

"Don't get lost in all that false hope, mother. It will be a waste of time and good energy."

"We'll see…" her mother ended their too-early-in-the-morning topic of conversation with those words, as she continued on her walk route at the end of Jacobi's driveway.

Jacobi never gave a second thought to bumping into Matt Huegen at the hospital. Something like that was just not on her radar. For years now, there's only been one man worth loving, despite the loneliness of never being able to call him her own. Until now. She thought of being with him again last night, and for the first time in her life she understood the desperation that led to sneaking around. She could only hope Marti was unaware of Ben's true whereabouts.

Her morning rounds at the hospital kept her insanely busy. When Jacobi finally sat down at her desk in her office at lunch time, Reeda interrupted her. "Keep eating, honey," Reeda told her as she saw her spooning yogurt into her mouth. "I'm not here on business."

"What else?" Jacobi reacted, dipping her spoon into her yogurt again. "More personal prying?"

Reeda smirked. "I don't think of it as that, especially when it's for your own good."

Jacobi kept eating to make it seem as if she was too pressed for time during her lunch break to have to listen to more judgement.

"My sister-in-law is a recovery nurse here." Her words hung in the air between them, and Jacobi could have thrown up her last swallow of yogurt, because she knew exactly where this was leading. "It seems one of her colleagues got an earful from Dr. Oliver's wife."

"I can only imagine," Jacobi quipped. "The things people say when they are coming off anesthesia shouldn't be taken too seriously."

"Well apparently she made a pretty serious accusation, directed at you."

"And what? Now the entire hospital thinks those two OBGYN's are getting hot and heavy in the stirrups?"

Reeda stifled a laugh. "I'd rather not know that part."

"There's nothing to know, Reeda. Gossip in any workplace always gets out of hand."

"This will get out of hand if you are not careful," she clearly warned her. "That poor woman though… with the miscarriages, the car accident, and now her marriage is in trouble."

"Right. Poor Marti."

"I'm not taking her side," Reeda was quick to clarify where she stood. "I only want to keep you from making a mistake that will lead to nothing but regret."

"How is it that you always make everything sound as if you are speaking from experience?"

"I'm older and wiser, that's how."

"I think there's more here that you are not saying."

"You're turning the tables so you won't have to be the one to face the music."

Jacobi shrugged.

"There was a doctor on staff here, before your time here. He was married with four children, and I had my own husband and crew at home. He and I worked the nightshift together. I knew what I was getting into. I'm not going to make excuses for my actions. All I'm trying to get across to you, by telling you this part of my past, is no matter how it feels at the time — it's a mistake and people are going to get hurt. Namely, yourself. Us women must look out for ourselves, and for each other."

"I appreciate what you're saying." Jacobi's expression was more relaxed than it looked a moment ago when she resented how Reeda was mothering her and judging her.

"Good," she smiled. "Now just don't let it go in one ear and out the other."

Jacobi laughed, because what the hell else was she going to do? One woman's past mistakes did not mean that she was doomed. She was in love with Ben. It was Marti who was the one on a path of destruction. If Jacobi took away anything from Reeda's lecture about people getting hurt, it was the fact that Marti needed to be stopped. And it was suddenly high time for Jacobi to face her again.

# Chapter 17

After work, Jacobi drove to Ben and Marti's house. She didn't let either of them know that she was coming over. She knew that Ben would be caught off guard, but she was going there unannounced regardless before she lost her nerve.

She waved to their neighbor, Dana who was standing in the middle of her own driveway as she drove by. When Jacobi got out of her car, she saw Dana crossing the street to get to her. "Hi there. How are you?" Jacobi called out to her first.

"Puzzled."

Jacobi watched her stare at the Oliver's house. "Why?"

"Ben left to go to the grocery store. He stopped me at my mailbox just to tell me that he would be gone for a little while. I suppose he wanted me to know that in case Marti needed something while he's gone. Anyway, the garage door over there is acting all willy nilly. I've been standing outside watching it go up and down, at least three times or so."

Since Jacobi had arrived and parked on the driveway, the double-car garage doors remained down. "Really? That's weird. Which side?"

"The rental van side." They leased a van for Marti following the accident that totaled hers.

"I'll go in and see what could be going on with that," Jacobi offered, and Dana started to back away.

"That would be great. I feel better knowing you're here. I didn't just want to ignore that, with Ben gone and all."

"Everyone needs an observant neighbor like you," Jacobi called after her as she walked up the sidewalk to the front door, and Dana laughed off the compliment.

She rang the doorbell and waited.

After ringing it once more, Jacobi tried the door handle and when it was unlocked, she went inside. That house had always felt like a second home to her. She wished that feeling remained and the awkwardness and shame wouldn't be present all the time now.

The living room and kitchen were empty, and when Jacobi was about to call out to them at the base of the stairs, she heard the hum of the garage door opening. She walked quickly through the house, into the kitchen, and then she pulled open the door that led out to the garage. Just as she stuck her head out first, the garage door began to close again. For a brief second, she thought she faintly smelled exhaust, and what she saw next was weird. Marti was sitting in the driver's seat of the van while Suzie stood on the passenger seat, leaning her little body over to hold onto the steering wheel and then reaching upward to press the button to open and close the garage door. Repeatedly.

When Marti saw Jacobi, she laughed. She wasn't startled or miffed. Apparently, only amused, as she stuck her head through the now open car window. Jacobi stepped down two steps and onto the garage floor. "What in the world are you two doing sitting in the van with the garage door down… or going up and down?"

"Just playing," Marti answered. It's a change of scenery for us since we're stuck at home all the time now."

"Where's Ben?" Jacobi asked her, despite already knowing that he had gone to the store.

"Is that why you're here?" Marti's face fell. "To see Ben?"

"No," Jacobi spoke the truth. "I just assumed he would be homebound with you."

"I sent him out for groceries, I'm just not ready to be seen in public yet." Jacobi already noticed from afar that the bandage was off. There was a pink line on her cheek that just looked sore when Jacobi wasn't up close to her to see anything more.

"Can we go inside to talk?" Jacobi asked as Suzie climbed over the seats, onto her mother's lap, and then she acted as if she wanted Jacobi to lift her through the open window.

"Sure," Marti agreed, as Jacobi grabbed and held Suzie for her. She watched her press her little hand to her own forehead and say, "head hurts." Jacobi creased her brow and looked at Marti. "She said her head hurts."

"Yeah, she lost her balance on the front seat and bumped her head on the console."

Jacobi studied the little one's face and eyes and wondered if that should be overlooked. Bumping her head again so soon after a mild concussion could cause further trouble. Marti opened the van door then and got out as Jacobi noticed that she had taken the keys out of the ignition and held them in her hand.

She looked down at them. "Why do you have your keys out here if you're not going anywhere?"

Marti shrugged. "I grabbed them out of habit, I guess."

Jacobi let it go, even though that also seemed strange.

When they went inside the house, Suzie seemed to be a bundle of energy again as she made her way to the living room to likely find a toy and bring it back to Jacobi. She stood just around the corner in the kitchen with Marti. "Tell me what brings you by," Marti asked her outright.

"I wanted to see how you're doing." That wasn't a lie.

"I'm okay. Having a sizeable scar on my face is taking some getting used to, but it will eventually be healed enough for me to conceal what only I'll be able to see without makeup."

"Thank goodness we are women. Makeup can bring us real comfort when we need it." Those were the kinds of things the two of them used to talk about when everything was a lot less complicated. As she said those words, which really were unimportant, Jacobi felt the awkward distance between them. And she believed that Marti did, too.

"I'm not so sure that makeup will be the thing that comforts me on nights like last night when I know that Ben is lying to me."

Jacobi's facial expression did not change.

"He told me that he was going to the hospital to catch up on paperwork, but he was with you, wasn't he?"

The uncertain thoughts which flooded her mind right now left Jacobi at a loss for what to say. She was not the type of person to back down from confrontation. It was her character to never be willing to compromise who she was or what she believed in. Not for anything or anyone. She had empathy and compassion, but she could hold her own. She understood more than anyone that life was what you made of it. While circumstances were not always fair, what was most important to Jacobi was how she carried herself.

"Ben is going to see you through your recovery," Jacobi told her, "but then he wants a life with me."

"Were you with him again last night?" Marti had every right to be hurt and angry, but there was something more in her eyes that startled Jacobi. She looked detached, as if someone could deliberately wave a hand in front of her face and she would not even react.

"Yes."

"Why are you here?" Marti appeared to surrender.

"Do you really need to ask me that question? I fear for that little girl's safety when she's alone with you. I haven't forgotten how you threatened me with her life. You need help, Marti."

"What I need is my family intact, and you are tearing us apart."

"I want you to talk to someone."

"I'm talking to you. It brings me inexplainable joy knowing that you know what I did and how it's tormenting you."

"You're sick," was all Jacobi could manage to utter. *Was there really anything left to say anymore?*

Jacobi's car had been parked on the driveway, blocking Ben's entrance to his side of the garage. Unbeknownst to them, Ben made his way inside the house through the front door, as he was juggling grocery bags. He closed the door with his foot and heard the two women in his life arguing in the kitchen. He started to move through the living room and dropped the bags at his feet when he saw Suzie slumped forward, her little body hanging over the side of the toybox. The thought that she could be asleep had not even crossed his mind; he immediately called out for her and ran to get to her.

Marti and Jacobi heard him say Suzie's name in an obvious state of panic, as they charged through the open doorway of the kitchen and around the corner. They had been too caught up in exchanging words with each other that they never thought to check on a child, to watch her while she was playing, to ensure that she was safe. It was a startling realization when they both saw Ben on the floor, checking her vitals. "What the hell happened here?" he screamed at them. "Call 911. Her breathing is so shallow!"

Jacobi was the first to have a phone in her hands and act quickly. All she could explain to the dispatcher was a child, two years old, had lost consciousness, she had a weak pulse, and her face was colorless. As she spoke into her phone, Jacobi watched Marti fall to her knees next to Ben. Their child, she was practically still a baby, was lifeless on the floor.

# Chapter 18

Jacobi sat alone in the waiting room in the ER. This was becoming an all-too-familiar place for all of them lately, and again she was beside herself with worry. She started to think about finding Marti in the garage, in the car with Suzie, and what that could have meant. Her mind was reeling when she looked up and saw Ben walking toward her.

She immediately stood up. "She's going to be okay," Ben kept his voice low because there were other people around them. Jacobi wasn't a crier, at least she did not cry very easily, but the moment she heard those words from him, relief filled her soul and a few tears spilled out of her eyes. Ben guided her down to the chair that she had been sitting on, and he wrapped his arm around her.

"I need you to explain to me exactly what happened. Marti told the doctor that Suzie bumped her forehead while playing, and a little while after she said that her head hurt. The doctor doesn't believe that she has another concussion, and the low oxygen level isn't adding up at all. They're going to run some tests, but she's awake and coherent and feeling a little fussy about keeping the oxygen mask on."

"Exactly what happened when I got there might explain this," she felt sick to her stomach as everything suddenly added up. The garage door opening and closing had gotten the attention of their neighbor, and then Jacobi found the two of them playing inside the van in the garage. She thought she faintly noticed the smell of exhaust. Marti had the keys in the ignition. *My God… what if she had not shown up the moment she did?* "Did Marti say where Suzie was playing when she bumped her head?"

"No, I don't think so. Why?"

"Dana was on the driveway when I got to your house. She told me that she saw one of your garage doors opening and closing. This went on for a little while, two or three times. The garage doors were both down when I got there, so I told her that I would see what was going on. I ended up finding Marti and Suzie playing in the van in the garage and the doors were closed. Ben, I think the van was running before I got there. Suzie probably had a headache from breathing in carbon monoxide."

Ben's face fell. "Oh my God."

"Marti is playing a dangerous game with Suzie's life, and she has to be stopped."

"You're coming with me," Ben stood up and pulled Jacobi to her feet along with him. Like it or not, Jacobi knew she had to be the one to stop Marti.

When Ben and Jacobi practically barged through the sliding door of the cubicle in the ER where Suzie was being treated, they found Marti cradling Suzie. She was perched on the gurney alongside her baby. Anyone else who witnessed that image would have been touched by a mother's love and genuine concern. Jacobi knew better, though, and she desperately needed Ben to finally be on her side.

"She's going to be okay," Marti spoke to Jacobi as if they were still the closest of friends. "I know you must feel as bad as I do about leaving her alone in the living room, believing that she was just playing and completely safe. I am beating myself up about that."

"Jacobi was able to clear up some of the confusion here," Ben spoke with no expression on his face."

"She was? How?"

Ben walked over to Marti and he helped her off the bed. He wasn't forceful, but he did physically move her away from their daughter. Jacobi stepped beside the bed, secured the railing on it, and she wanted to stay right there to comfort Suzie. "You never said that Suzie hit her head while playing in the van. You left out that part from your story. You also didn't mention that you had the engine running in our closed garage. Please explain that to me." His voice was calm but demanding.

"That's not what happened," Marti was quick to defend herself.

"No?" Ben was persistent, and Jacobi thought to herself, *finally!* "We've never let her play in the van while it was parked inside the garage. She's two years old! Things can happen. What I really do not understand is why you had the engine running. I went out to the store because you aren't ready to be in public yet. Why would you start up the van if you were not going anywhere?"

"I don't know. I guess I wasn't thinking. Suzie was pressing the garage door button, making it go up and down. So, there was air circulating if that's what you are insinuating."

"Our child had a headache and then she passed out. She had been in a parked car, running periodically in a closed garage. All of that points directly to asphyxiation, and when the doctor hears about this, the police will in turn have to be notified."

Marti's eyes widened. "I am her mother. I would never do anything to harm her. I resent your accusations. You're taking all of this out of context. Were you there? No. So it's Jacobi's word against mine? You're choosing her over your own family again."

"I'm choosing to protect my daughter from harm. From *you*."

Jacobi was trying to distract Suzie on the bed with her phone by playing a video of a cartoon, which did captivate her attention. What was happening in that cubicle right now was simultaneously awful and unbelievable and disheartening. Jacobi was stunned silent, watching them. The moment that Marti realized she had lost, that her husband was going to take their child away from her, that her freedom was suddenly uncertain, she unraveled in front of them. She backed her body against the wall and sunk down to the floor. She pulled her legs up to her chest and began to tremble. "It was raining," she spoke as if she was in somewhat of a trance. I knew you agreed to come home, but things were going to be different. How could they be the same if you're sleeping in the guest room and counting the days until you could leave me. I - I - I," she stuttered and began to cry. Her fair skin was blotchy, making the pink scar on her face more prominent. She roughly feathered both of her hands through the blonde ringlets on her head, leaving them disheveled as she was able to find her words again. "I couldn't take the thought of you and Jacobi moving on with my child and having more children. Babies that I can't seem to have anymore." Marti choked on a sob, and Jacobi tried to hold herself together. "I couldn't see the road in front of me when I was driving that day. I kept struggling to keep the van between the lines. I started to cross over, I knew it, and suddenly it occurred to me that I could set you free only if I left this world... with Suzie."

Jacobi watched Ben close his eyes and force back his emotions. "And in the rental van today? Did you think the two of you could just breathe in poison, fall asleep, and painlessly die? Did you once even think about me coming home to find that scene at our house? She's my child, too!" he tried very hard to keep his voice down, but this time he couldn't. And he choked on a sob that he tried to jam back down his throat as he spat those words at her.

"I wanted more babies," she rehashed that truth, and it was suddenly clear how two devastating miscarriages had been the beginning of her downfall. "Then, you changed your mind about babies and about me and our family. You chose her." Marti never made eye contact with Jacobi. "I couldn't handle anything else. Two awful miscarriages broke me. And then you did, Ben."

"You need professional help," were the only words that he could manage to say once Marti revealed her torment.

"No. I don't want a shrink," she shook her head adamantly. "It's not going to help me to confess anything to a stranger. How could it? I've admitted everything to you... and that's how you look at me. You are the only one who matters to me. Can you not see that?"

"So what am I supposed to do?" Ben asked his wife, the mother of his child, a woman that he once genuinely loved. Jacobi felt the sadness that she heard in his words to her. "I can't trust that you will not hurt her," he glanced at Suzie, and he was grateful that she was too little to understand what was happening between her parents. "Tell me where I should go from here?"

"I'll be the one to go," she suddenly sounded sensible. That was really the most difficult part of this. One moment she was crazed and the next she was the same ole Marti they knew and loved. "I can't handle a psych ward or a prison. Please. Just let me go.

"I can't do that," Ben responded. "I couldn't live with myself knowing that I never tried to help you."

"Don't pretend that I matter to you now," Marti called him out.

Jacobi reached for the call button to get the nurse in there. The moment they heard the voice on the other line ask if everything was alright, Jacobi spoke. "We need some help in here."

Ben spun his head around to face Jacobi. He had questions in his eyes, but he never spoke. At the same time, Marti put her face in her hands on the floor and surrendered.

"If you can't do it, I will," Jacobi spoke quietly. There was a part of her that wanted this unstable woman out of all their lives. But deep in her soul what she wanted more was for someone to reach her and heal her. It was devastating to see the pain that motivated Marti's actions.

# Chapter 19

The trained professionals for acute psychiatric conditions were summoned to the emergency room. A few things occurred as Marti was being detained. She lashed out at Jacobi, accusing her of taking everything from her. *Her husband. Her child. Her entire life and her reason to live.* Suzie had already been carried out of the room by a nurse and she had been visibly upset not to have her mommy or daddy or even Jacobi holding her and walking away. Jacobi was escorted out of there as well. Since Marti made it abundantly clear that Jacobi was the culprit for her distress, a nurse nudged her by the elbow and led her out. She never had the chance to even look at Ben. She also wanted so badly to comfort Suzie, but now she couldn't find her. Everything had suddenly happened so fast once Jacobi called for help.

Ben stayed with Marti.

Jacobi ended up walking the hospital halls. She was still wearing her scrubs, because once she was off duty she had gone directly to Ben and Marti's house. It felt surreal to her knowing that she had shown up and gone in the garage when Marti was setting the stage to take her life and her child's. She was overwhelmed just thinking about it now.

She thought about going home, but Ben was still there. And, if he or Suzie needed her, she wanted to be close. She opted to stay in the building and moved toward the elevator to take it up to the OB floor. She could hide out in her office until she was able to reach Ben or hear from him first.

She crossed her arms over her chest as she stood and waited for the elevator that would be going up. When the tone dinged and the doors opened, she was face to face with Matt Huegen. The new hire from her past that her mother couldn't wait to tell her about this morning.

*You may wanna look him up and purposely fall into his path!*

And there he was right in front of her now. While it had been seventeen years since she saw him last, he still looked like the Matt she remembered. Tall, lean, light brown hair and dark blue eyes. He did have facial hair now, which was a well-manicured, closely-shaved beard. He had aged somewhat, but instead of appearing touched by FatherTime, he looked distinguished. Perhaps that had something to do with the white lab coat he was wearing.

"Reese?"

She tried to smile, to pretend she had not just walked away from a scene that resembled hell on earth. "Matt Huegen... this could not be more unexpected." The fact that he was in the building was not a surprise because of her mother's forewarning, but his timing did catch her off guard. She only wanted to be alone in her office and not have to make eye contact or speak to anyone along the way.

"I'd be lying if I said I didn't know you were Dr. Jacobi, OBGYN on Floor 6."

She laughed. "And you're?"

"A doctor of sports medicine. Floor 3."

He made her laugh again, and she noticed that he stalled the elevator as they were currently in limbo. No one was going up or down as long as this conversation lasted.

"Are you coming or going, for a shift?"

"I'm... I don't know," she paused. "Long story. Long day. I actually just came from the ER."

"I hope everything is alright."

"No, it's not, but I won't burden you with my problems. It was good to see you though." She would just back away and take the stairs instead.

"Reese?"

She had yet to step away from the open elevator door.

"Would you like to grab a cup of coffee in the cafeteria? Maybe you need to talk about it? I'm still an objective listener."

~

They sat at a corner table with two paper cups of black coffee. Matt added cream and sugar to his, while Jacobi liked hers black. He bought her coffee, and she felt a little awkward when he offered. Ben always bought her coffee whenever they were able to take a break in the cafeteria together.

She was quiet, and Matt studied her briefly before he spoke. "Your hands are trembling."

"Oh," she looked down. "Yeah, I guess the shock of everything is wearing off. A body's delayed reactions to distress can be strange sometimes."

"If you weren't the one in need of urgent care in the ER today, who was?"

She shook her head. "I don't know where to begin, or if I should even try to put this into words. I mean, I don't really talk about it with anyone. Just Ben."

Matt looked at her hands. He had already noted that she was not wearing a wedding ring. The fact that she used her given name as a doctor had not really sealed that burning question for him, so he had asked around at the hospital. He found out a few things along with his inquiry. She and a male doctor, who she had gone to medical school alongside, were the dynamic duo on the obstetrics floor. *They would make a great couple,* one of the sports medicine PA's had shared her observation with Matt. And another chimed in that *there was no way the two of them weren't sleeping together.* But then Matt heard that Dr. Ben Oliver was a married man.

"Is he your colleague in OB?"

Jacobi should have been surprised, but she knew word got around in that hospital or in any work environment for that matter. Drama and gossip thrived wherever there were human beings. "Yes, we've been in each other's lives since med school. His wife and little girl are like family to me." She could have thrown up as she said those words. *Look what she had done to the people she claimed to care about.*

"So was it Ben that you were in the ER with?"

"No. His little girl. Her name is Suzie and she's two years old."

"Was there an accident?"

Jacobi sighed. "Do you want me to start from the beginning?" She seriously contemplated telling him everything. Maybe it was time that she talked about it. What would it matter now if he, in turn, told someone else? Word was going to spread anyway. Everything that went down in that ER would be whispered about.

"I have time." The sincerity in his eyes was so convincing that Jacobi caved. She told him about the way she and Ben had always fought their feelings… and kept the secret about their night together just hours before his wedding day. She admitted to harboring her feelings for him the last several years and telling herself that work was enough for her. Being an integral part of his family's life had also filled a void for her. She explained how Ben's wife had multiple miscarriages and emotionally started to spiral. And then she confessed how she and Ben recently began having an affair and he was going to leave his wife. Jacobi explained that after she and Ben slept together, she told his wife the truth. Her mental state crashed after that. Matt's eyes widened when Jacobi told him about Marti's suicide attempts with herself and her child. The latest one, asphyxiation, had been today. Also, just a short time ago in that ER, Ben's wife was detained and brought to the psychiatric ward in the basement of Cleveland Clinic. Saying all of that out loud really hadn't helped. Jacobi was fighting back the tears now.

Matt reached for her hand. "I am so sorry. Gosh, all of that is a lot to absorb. It's no wonder you're reeling."

"So you're not going to judge me?" she halfheartedly teased him. But the truth was, she really wasn't one to care what other people thought. She lived for herself.

"No, and no one else should either. I still see what I've always seen in you, Reese Jacobi. There's no one more genuine. What we see is what we get."

"Like it or not," she tried to laugh.

"What's not to like?" he smiled.

"I didn't think I would, but I actually do feel relieved after talking about this. Thank you for those great listening ears."

He nodded. "Anytime."

She had barely sipped her coffee, and now she pushed it forward on the table between them.

"So what's your next move?" he asked her, wondering how the circumstances would change things for her and the doctor that she was in love with.

## Nothing Left to Give

"I have to talk to Ben. There's just a lot of uncertainty. Namely, what's going to happen to Marti?"

"I think any other woman would snag this chance to be with the love of her life." Matt's words were straightforward, and Jacobi didn't know what to say, other than the truth that had been circling in her mind ever since she left Marti and Ben in the ER with those people dressed in white who intervened, probably with a straitjacket in tow. Jacobi didn't even want to imagine that struggle.

"How do we move on from something like that?" She was afraid of that answer.

"I don't know. Time heals, I guess. Or, if anything, we learn a new way to cope and carry on. No one knows what you want better than you do. You'll figure it out."

She smiled at him for the umpteenth time this evening. He was so easy to be with. This time she caught herself searching his hand for a wedding band. And he saw her.

He held up both hands in the air. "Never married. Just a broken engagement." She stifled a giggle because he was smiling, and his eyes looked bluer in the bad lighting at that corner table.

"She's out there, I'm sure of it. A man with attentive listening skills should never be unattached."

He laughed out loud.

And that's when she stood up, took ahold of her coffee cup, and said she had to leave now.

He pointed to the cup in her hand, as he followed her to stand up. "That's likely cold. Throw it out. And let me know when I can buy you another round sometime."

# Chapter 20

Again, Jacobi never made it to her office. This time, she made it onto the elevator when Ben called her.

"Where are you?" he asked.

"Here in the hospital."

"I'm in the parking lot. I'm taking Suzie home." Jacobi sighed in relief, knowing that her oxygen levels had to be normal again. "Will you meet us there?"

~

Ben was holding Suzie in his arms when he opened the front door for Jacobi to come inside. Jacobi reached for Suzie, badly wanting to hold that little girl tightly and forever keep her safe. "Can I hold you?" Jacobi's voice cracked, and Suzie leaned into her. She kissed the top of her head, again burying her nose into her soft, spiral curls. *She was Marti's mini.* And, sadly, that truth felt incredibly painful now.

"I want mommy."

Jacobi shared a look with Ben.

"I know you do, and I promise we will go see mommy very soon," Ben tried to reassure her. "Remember she's feeling sick and needs to spend a little time in the hospital."

"To get better?" It was a simple, innocent question from a child and two grown adults were at a loss for an answer.

"The doctors are going to try very hard to get mommy well again." The sadness in Ben's voice broke Jacobi's heart. There was no definite answer. No one knew if Marti would ever return to herself again. And even if medication and counseling could bring her back, irreversible damage had already been done. She could not be trusted alone with Suzie ever again. Her rights as a mother were now nonexistent. All of that weighed on Jacobi's mind.

Jacobi stayed for Suzie's nighttime routine. She took a bath. She got dressed in her favorite pink pjs, and the Ben read her a bedtime story before he tucked her in. Jacobi stood in the doorway listening, and when Suzie called her over for a kiss goodnight, she was grateful for the darkened room so no one would see the tears in her eyes.

## Nothing Left to Give

Downstairs, Ben sat on the sofa and Jacobi paced the hardwood floor in front of him. "I can't relax my mind," she admitted. "I keep replaying what happened here... and then in the ER."

"All I know is if you hadn't shown up here when you did... my little girl would be gone."

"And so would Marti," Jacobi added.

"She doesn't deserve to live," his words were cold and callous. In his defense, his anger was valid. His wife had tried to end their little girl's life. *Twice.*

"Nothing good will come from meeting her anger with your own." Jacobi was trying very hard not to succumb to her own repulsion for Marti's actions.

"She fought them when they tried to move her downstairs to the psych ward." Those two words together were extremely difficult to speak, and it was even worse to imagine it. "They ended up sedating her."

"What happens from here?" Jacobi's question could have pertained to a lot of things right now.

"I need to find someone to care for Suzie while I work. I'm going to start with Dana, but it's not like she runs a daycare across the street. I thought about the daycare center adjacent to the hospital, because then I'd be close by."

"I understand your eagerness to fill the voids right now," Jacobi chose her words carefully. "I know you depended so much on Marti to always be with Suzie, and now you're scrambling to make things work out. You need to take a minute to process what happened, Ben."

"I have processed it," his words were unwavering. "Marti lost her right to be a mother to Suzie." Ben would not seek criminal charges against her; he just wanted her out of their lives.

"But you just promised Suzie that she would see her soon?"

"She's little. She'll—"

"Don't," Jacobi interrupted him. "Don't you dare say that she will forget about Marti. There is no amount of time that will ever keep her from remembering that she has a mother, or from missing her terribly."

"So what do you suggest I do instead? You're the one who warned me that Marti was a danger to Suzie, beginning with the car wreck that wasn't really an accident. And it was you who saved her from closing her eyes and dying in the garage. Do you really want me to allow Marti to be a part of our lives still?"

"Of course I don't want to ever risk Suzie's life being in danger," Jacobi strongly defended herself. "But Marti is sick. She needs help. And, maybe, her chances of getting well will depend on whether or not she feels abandoned and alone."

"Then you go see her!" Ben snapped at her.

"Right. The friend showing up who robbed her of everything should go over well." Jacobi's tone was snarky.

"See, you don't have all the answers either."

"I know you're hurting," Jacobi resisted the urge to sit down beside him on the sofa. "Just try to keep an open mind. As long as Marti is getting medical treatment, there's no risk involved concerning Suzie. You and I are doctors, Ben. We see how things can and do go wrong with the female human body every day. The mind is no different."

"I can't," was all he said, as Jacobi realized that the two of them may never see eye to eye on this. It's not as if Jacobi had forgiven Marti. She didn't even know if that were possible. And she certainly wouldn't be able to forget the harm that she was capable of unleashing on her own child. But something changed for Jacobi when she watched Marti's body in a fetal position on the floor, when she was at her absolute lowest. Weakness, pain, and devastation had wreaked havoc on her body, her mind, and her soul. *Was there any turning back following that?*

She turned away from Ben to retrieve her purse on the dining room table. "Are you leaving? I know it will look bad when word gets out about Marti," he didn't want to think about that now, "but I thought you would stay with us? At least for tonight?"

This time it was Jacobi's turn to say, "I can't."

# Chapter 21

Jacobi closed the door to her office. She arrived much earlier than she typically did each morning, which was purposeful today, so she would not have to make an entrance in front of a full staff. She expected Reeda to be the first to have already heard the news from the ER staff last night. And of course she would want to talk about it.

An hour later, there was a knock on her door while it swung open. Jacobi looked up from her desk and her eyes widened when she saw Ben.

"What are you doing here?"

"I work here," he smirked.

"I thought you would need time."

"I needed to be here. Now let's go, you're coming with me."

"Where? I'll have patients in 15 minutes."

"This won't take long. I've asked our staff to gather in the conference room. I just want to get this out in the open so we can both bypass the awkward."

"Christ, Ben. Thanks for the warning."

He chuckled, as they walked side by side, together, which was exactly how they were going to face this.

Ben closed the door and Jacobi scanned the long, rectangular table that filled the middle of the room. She tried not to look at faces, but she did anyway. She stayed strong, and she felt stronger when she caught Reeda's eye and she winked at her.

"Looks like we are all here," Ben addressed the room. "I know we have patients waiting, so I will make this quick and hopefully painless. Dr. Jacobi and I have been dealing with something personal. You've all heard the rumors and have been whispering around yourselves so here goes my story. Our story," he added, and glanced at Jacobi, but she forced her expression not to change.

"My wife, Marti has been silently struggling with some mental health issues that began when she and I lost two babies in the last year. The miscarriages and the fact that I recently told her that I wanted out of our marriage have taken a huge toll on her," Ben glanced at Jacobi.

"I know what you are all thinking," Jacobi interjected. "Let me take this for a moment," she looked at Ben. "Dr. Oliver and I have crossed the boundaries of our friendship and working relationship. That said, we did not hide it from Marti. I told her the truth."

"My wife's instability caused her to try to take her own life as well as our daughter's," Ben confirmed what most of them already knew, but it was still difficult for him to say out loud, and for them to hear. "The car accident in the rainstorm several days ago and our van's engine running in our closed garage yesterday were both attempts by Marti to end her own life and Suzie's." There were a few gasps, but mainly everyone had already processed that horrible story. "Suzie is fine, thank goodness. And Marti," he paused, "is a patient downstairs in the psychiatric unit." Ben paused again, and Jacobi remained standing by his side. "So, that's the awful truth of my life currently. I just wanted you all to hear it from me. Judge all you want, just don't do it on company time. Dr. Jacobi and I, as always, will be putting our patients first when we are inside these hospital walls. What she and I decide to do with our personal lives is our business. I will say, with all of you as my witnesses," he smiled, "that I do hope Dr. Jacobi and I have a future together."

Jacobi was speechless. That part, she was not expecting. She cleared her throat and did not look Ben's way. Instead, she faced her people. "That wasn't a proposal," she quipped, and a little laughter erupted. "My priority is my patients. That will not change for me. I will make no apologies for the choices in my personal life. Not here. That doesn't pertain to here. Do I have regrets? Of course I do. I wish that those who love Marti could have seen her downward spiral before she took those drastic measures."

"That's all," Ben concluded. "Back to work everyone."

A few of the employees reached out to Ben as they walked by, offering their thoughts, good vibes, and prayers for his wife...

# Nothing Left to Give

and many mentioned how they were grateful that Suzie was alright. They weren't just coworkers, they cared about each other like family. Last in line, Reeda propped her hand on the open door when she looked back. Both Jacobi and Ben held her eye contact. "I don't know if I've ever been prouder of you two," was all she said before she closed the door behind her.

"And I don't know how to take that," Ben spoke the moment they were alone.

"I do," Jacobi told him. "We faced the music. You got up here and you told the truth about Marti, and you also admitted your own wrongdoing."

"I'm glad you were brave with me," he meant those words.

"We all make mistakes, Ben. Why pretend we're perfect?"

"You and I were not a mistake."

Jacobi stared at him for a moment before she turned on her heels and left the room. Ben was the last man standing in there, and he couldn't help but feel a little defeated. There was something different between them now, and he was afraid of how that wedge felt.

~

At the end of the workday, Jacobi left the sixth floor quickly. She made a phone call during her lunch break to see if the psychiatric ward allowed visitors. One per day, she was told, and she forewarned them to expect her late this afternoon for Marti Oliver.

She took the elevator all the way down to the hospital's basement. The thought freaked her out a little, but she never let her fear show in any situation, and she wasn't about to start now.

She checked in at the main desk, and then she was directed to a sterile room with white walls, white floors, no wall hangings and no furniture except for a square table with four chairs. She was told that they would bring Marti to her.

And, five minutes later, they did.

She stood in the doorway without moving into the room at first. With a slight nudge from the guard, who said he would be waiting right outside the door, she reluctantly entered the room. Jacobi stared at her. She couldn't help it. She wore what looked like a pale blue cotton jumpsuit, likely the same type that prisoners wore in orange. Her face was makeup less and her hair was unkempt, which made her blonde curls look even wilder.

"I get one visitor a day and it's you?" Marti's tone was snarky as she sat down across from Jacobi at the small table. The pink scar on her face was the blatant reminder of what Marti had done to herself and to her life.

"Better than no visitors at all," Jacobi snapped back.

"Why are you here?" she sounded defeated.

"I wanted to see for myself that you are getting help."

"Because Ben won't come?"

"I want to talk about you, not Ben."

"Me. Hmm. Let's see. I've willingly agreed to take a strong medication that one of the head shrinks prescribed. *See how you feel*, she said, *it may give you some clarity*. You know, less dark thoughts and more unicorns and rainbows."

Jacobi stifled a laugh.

"And guess what?" Marti asked her. "I do have a clearer head today, but the downside of that is my conscience is about to do me in. I hurt my child. I tried to end her life. What kind of monster does something like that? Twice! I don't deserve to be a mother. Perhaps that's why God took back my other babies before I had the chance to give birth to them. And now I've lost my little girl, too."

Her remorse had to count for something. But, Jacobi forced herself to keep a level head. Marti was a master at manipulating. She had done as much following the car accident, which was why Ben didn't want to believe that she crossed the line and endangered their lives on purpose.

"So what happens now?" Jacobi asked her outright. "Do you want to get well?"

"I don't see the point," Marti was quick with her response. "I mean, I've lost my entire life. You've taken most of it, actually." That was a clue for Jacobi. Marti still dwelled on blaming someone other than herself. Repeatedly damning Jacobi seemed to be her coping mechanism. The anger and the hatred seemed to fuel her.

"What's the alternative then? To sulk the days away in a nuthouse?"

Marti glared at her. "Why does it concern you?"

"I wish it didn't," Jacobi admitted. "I should be telling myself that it's only a matter of time before Ben divorces you. And then of course there's Suzie. I could effortlessly slip right into the role of being her mommy. Sure, those two are both hurting, and they will always wonder why you did what you did to them, but in time we could all move on together and be happy." Jacobi saw the hurt in Marti's eyes as she painted that picture for her, and told a story of moving on and forgetting about her. Eventually, she would just be a bad memory that only surfaced now and then. "But that's not what I'm doing. I'm here because I'm struggling with how I can save you from yourself. There's potential for a recovery. Who knows? You could work your way to having supervised visitation with your child. *If* you get well. *If* you work hard to fight those demons that transformed a perfectly sane person into a madwoman. The thing is though, Marti, *you* have to want it."

Jacobi stood up, pushed in her chair, and backed away from the table. She hoped that her words would somehow reach Marti, but there was no guarantee anymore with her. She wasn't convinced that showing up there today was her best idea. At least not until she tapped on the door and was able to get the guard's attention when she peered through the small window. As she was being let out of there, Marti called her name.

Jacobi looked back when Marti spoke to her.

"Thank you for coming."

# Chapter 22

Ben returned a phone call to the doctor in charge of Marti's case. He was informed that she agreed to take medication, and once daily she would be evaluated by a psychiatrist to determine any fluctuations in her mental state. The only additional news that the doctor had to report was the reminder that Marti was allowed one visitor per day.

"I doubt she'll be getting any visitors anytime soon." It sounded harsh, coming from her husband, but Ben was not about to sit down for small talk with her. There was no getting past the awful truth of what she had done to Suzie.

"Actually, she had one today," the doctor responded.

"She did?" Ben spoke into the phone with a puzzled look on his face.

"A woman about the same age as Marti. Tall, dark hair. She was wearing hospital scrubs, and it was mentioned that she works here at Cleveland Clinic. I could look up her name on the check-in list, if you'd like?"

There was no need for that. Ben knew exactly who paid Marti a visit. He ended the call with the physician and made another one.

Jacobi was at home when she saw the caller ID for Ben's incoming call.

"Hi," was all she said to him when she answered.

"I have a question for you," he spoke as a matter of fact, as she waited in silence because she knew what was coming. "Why did you do it? What was your motive behind going to see Marti after everything she's done?"

"No motive. Just compassion. Or maybe I'm still trying to figure out what the hell happened to a perfectly well-rounded, good human being."

"Nothing can undo what she did."

"Right. But in order for me to be able to move forward, I can't be cruel to her. Yes, I believe that she needs help and that she should be kept away from Suzie unless it's a supervised visit. But I can't be on board with punishing her with abandonment. She will lose herself for sure if we all just drop her like she never even mattered."

"What did you take away from your visit with her?"

"She appears to be remorseful and very hard on herself," Jacobi gave him an honest, forthright answer. "She also continues to harbor anger and resentment, namely toward me."

"Did it upset her to have you there?"

"I think she wanted me to believe that was the case, at first, but it also seemed like she chose to let me in to feel a little less alone."

"I don't understand how the two of you could possibly carry on a friendship now."

"It's far from a friendship anymore."

"Then what are you doing?"

"Trying to help."

"For Marti's sake or your own?" Ben may have been onto her now.

"A little of both," she confessed. "I don't want to have this guilt strapped to my back for the rest of my life. It's not my fault that you fell out of love with your wife. I'm also not to blame for the harm that Marti brought to Suzie. But I am the one who led her on this downward spiral when I thought telling her about us would be something that she could handle. I mean, did I actually expect her to bow out gracefully from her life as she's known it? What woman can handle discovering that her husband shares a deeper, stronger love with someone else?"

"Nothing is going to change any of that now."

"Do you really think, even with the right help, that it's too late for Marti to save herself?"

"I don't know, but if you don't stay out of it, she's going to take you down with her."

"That's overdramatic, don't you think?"

"Do you see what you're doing?" Ben tried to ignore the panic rising in his chest. He hated the distance that this was putting between them. "You're choosing Marti over us. Why include her anymore? She should be completely out of our lives, by fault of her own. Just let it be."

When they ended their call, nothing felt right between them.

~

Forty-eight hours went by. They had both been busy delivering babies in the middle of the night. Two nights ago, three of Jacobi's patients delivered in the wee hours of the morning. And last night, Ben got a call after midnight because a patient's water had broken. Gone were the days of being able to run out, leaving Marti to hold down the fort at home with Suzie. His life was already so different, and he cursed it. He wanted to call on Jacobi for help, but she had gotten very little sleep the previous night, or she also could be called in to work. This time, he relied on his neighbor, but he swore to her and to himself that he needed to have a permanent plan in place.

He had just enough time to go home to take a shower and then wake Suzie for daycare before he needed to be back at work. Sleep would have to wait, but he was feeling exhausted and short tempered by the time he returned to the hospital. He went into the locker room before going to his office, and in there he saw Jacobi changing from one pair of scrubs to another. He stared before he spoke. "It's rude to gawk at a woman when she's half naked."

He laughed. "Did you just get here?"

"About an hour and a half ago. I had an emergency C-section" That explained why she needed a change of scrubs. "I heard you were here around midnight."

He nodded.

"Why the scowl?" She was completely dressed now, having covered the parts of her body that Ben had already seen, touched, and known all too well.

"I had to ask Dana in the middle of the night to come over and be in the house while Suzie slept. I need a good plan in place. When I have an emergency, I have to be able to just go."

"You're mad because that used to be so easy with Marti."

"Yeah," he agreed. "I am mad. I don't want to be a single dad. I wanted to co-parent with her."

"You could have called me, you know," she offered.

"But you ended up here, too. It defeats the purpose to have my backup person also be on call for babies who cannot wait until morning to be born."

Jacobi agreed. "I do want to help when I can. You know that."

"Thank you," Ben met his eyes with hers.

"You're welcome," she smiled at him.

"We're going to get this right," his confidence was infectious, and Jacobi wanted to believe him.

Before she had the chance to respond, Reeda barged through the locker room door. The woman always made an entrance, no matter if it was urgent or not.

"Dr. Oliver, do you have your cell phone on you?" He reached into both pockets of his pants.

"Damn it. I must have left it in the car."

"They called from downstairs. It's Marti. Something's going on and you're needed."

He spun his head around and Jacobi was standing there, wide-eyed and worried. How could they not think what they were thinking? Ben had been assured that she would be watched closely, but that might not have mattered as Marti clearly knew how to outsmart people.

"Did they say why? Reeda, come on! You asked, didn't you?"

"No. You know darn well they didn't say anything to me over the phone. I'm just the messenger and you need to move it to go see what's going on. She's still your wife. You are obligated to go."

Ben left in a hurry, while Jacobi thought to call after him, but she didn't even know what to say. She was so scared that this time Marti had gone all the way.

Reeda remained standing at the door after Ben was gone. She saw the fear in Jacobi's eyes.

"I should have checked on her the past two days. I meant to, but it's been crazy busy here. No one else visits her, I don't think. She must have felt so alone…" Jacobi was obviously jumping to terrible conclusions.

"You need to stop that," Reeda scolded her. "Whatever has happened, it's not your doing."

"What time is my first patient?"

"In 45 minutes."

"I need some air. I'm just going to step outside."

Reeda nodded. "Maybe look up to the heavens and say a prayer or two that this already sad story didn't just get worse."

# Chapter 23

Jacobi sat down on a backless concrete bench on the hospital grounds. This was arrival time for many of the employees who were beginning their day shift. Only a few minutes passed before Jacobi heard someone call her by her first name. Other than with her mother, she just didn't answer to *Reese* anymore.

She looked and there again was her old buddy, Matt. "Hey, good morning," she gave him her best smile, despite the worry that clouded her mind.

"How good is it?" he asked her, as he wondered if something sad had happened with one of her patients or a baby. "You look miles away right now."

He was able to read her well, and that simply felt nice. That's what friends did, and quite frankly Jacobi didn't have too many of those anymore. Her life had been all about Ben and Marti for years. They were the prominent members of her adult circle.

"I don't know how much you've heard," she paused, and stood up from the bench. It just felt weird having him standing over her to talk.

"Pretty much all of it," Matt admitted. "Even the part where Dr. Oliver proposed to you in front of the entire staff."

She rolled her eyes at the way reality was often embellished when a story was told from person to person. "Not a proposal, more like a declaration of love."

"I see," Matt nodded. "So, the two of you are planning a life together?"

"I don't think that would be appropriate right now, considering…"

"Right. Yeah. I know. I guess what I'm asking is, are you as certain of your future as he is?"

"I want to be," she answered. "All of this has just been a lot to take in."

"I don't know if you remember that I played football in high school," he began, and she laughed out loud at the spontaneity of his comment.

"You kissed me on the bleachers after a Friday night game," she was still giggling, partially because she felt awkward.

"I did, didn't I?" he grinned.

"Why are we talking about that now?" she teetered with being borderline embarrassed.

"My coach back then... Coach Kauling... he said something to us once as a team, and it stuck with me for life. If you're going to do something, do it now. If you have something to say, don't wait until it's too late. Seize opportunity when it presents itself."

Jacobi listened intently, and she questioned whether or not she had lived like that. When it came to Ben, the answer was both yes and no.

"So how would you apply that to your life now?" she asked him. "You've landed a great job here, furthering your medical career. I'd say that's being proactive when opportunity knocks."

"I couldn't be in a better place professionally," he agreed. "It's my personal life that I need to grab by the horns and steer it in another direction other than going nowhere."

She smiled at him. "For me, it's always been Ben. I really do think I would have waited forever, alone, and knowing I would never have him, if it wasn't for the major changes in our lives lately."

Jacobi could see some disappointment in Matt's expression, and she wasn't quite sure how to read that.

"What's funny about life is sometimes we see ourselves going one way and we end up completely turned around, somewhere else, and we're happy because that's how it was really supposed to be." His words were accurate.

"Life works like that sometimes, doesn't it," she laughed a little.

"I'd like to find out if it could... for us, I mean," Matt's words were blunt and Jacobi was flattered, but not taken in. "Have a drink with me... or dinner? No expectations. Just seizing an opportunity to reconnect? What do you say... yes?"

Jacobi smiled. It just wasn't possible for her to imagine herself with anyone else but Ben. And she had always wondered if that was a blessing or a curse. He had consumed her heart for sure.

"Matt Huegen, the football stud from high school... you can do better than a woman whose heart is already taken."

He laughed to ease this awkwardness of being turned down, but he wished with all of his heart that Reese Jacobi had felt differently.

"I need to get back inside," she initiated for them to part ways.

"I'll walk you to the elevator."

"Matt?" she spoke as he stepped ahead of her to hold the door that someone just pulled opened. He looked back at her. "Do you want the best advice that I can possibly give at this stage in my life?"

"Sure," he smiled, and his eyes looked as blue as she remembered.

"Don't wait. Don't allow anything to fester in your heart for too long. Seize life but know that some opportunities are simply not meant to be."

Matt pretended to wipe his brow. "Ah you're killing me," they both laughed out loud. "Can a grown man die of sheer disappointment?"

"I can help you easily forget that you ever thought we had a chance," she suggested and he frowned a little.

"How?"

"I'm pregnant with Ben's baby."

~

Ben was directed into a room where a man in a business suit sat at a table, which was the only piece of furniture in the sterile, all white, room. "Who are you?" he asked as he stepped inside, not really knowing what, or who, he expected to find.

"I'm your wife's attorney."

Ben wasn't aware that Marti had an attorney. "What happened to her?" he asked, and there was urgency in his voice.

"She came to her senses," Marti spoke for herself from the doorway, where a guard stood behind her. Ben spun his head around at the sound of her voice.

"Marti? What's going on here?" He couldn't deny his relief in seeing her alive. He really had feared that she was gone. Maybe this was his awakening in the sense that he still cared about her.

He watched her walk over to her attorney and take a seat beside him. "Sit down, Ben. There are some things that we need to finalize." This was his wife, through and through. Confident and in control. She was the woman that somehow had a way of forcing the stars to be aligned. But she was also the same person who connived and fought like hell when things did not go her way. And that clearly had been her downfall.

"I don't understand the emergency here," he was clearly annoyed.

"It's not like you were going to ever stop by," she called him out. "I'll get right to the point of this. I hired a lawyer and filed for a divorce. I also have been granted a transfer to a facility in Michigan. It's top-notch and noted for its success with mental health patients. I want to get better, Ben. I want to somehow be a part of Suzie's life again."

Ben watched her expression closely. He wanted to believe her, but he made that mistake before. She was good at being believable. "Why the divorce? I think it's fair for me to say that I thought you would put up a fight for our marriage."

"Yes, but that was before I threw it all away." She sounded so rational that Ben found it difficult not to be taken in. "I need to be the one to set you free, because I know that's where we are now. I also want a chance to make things right with myself first... and eventually with my daughter. I am being transferred this afternoon."

"This all seems sudden?" Ben questioned her motive.

"You try to sit in a padded room for 72 hours and not think about how badly you want to put one foot in front of the other to begin to make changes for the better with your life."

"What are those papers asking of me?" Ben directed his question to the businessman seated beside her. "Other than the end of our marriage, I want the facts. I also will have a lawyer, of my own, take a look before I sign anything."

"Your wife is requesting to have supervised visitation rights once she reaches that point in her recovery. This divorce agreement will be null and void without your consent on that."

Ben shook his head as if he was going to stop the proceeding, here and now. "Of course, there's a catch."

"I am her mother," Marti spoke in her own defense.

"You sure as hell didn't protect her like a mother should," he retaliated. The pain in his voice was what kept Marti serene. The damage she had done was all too real and heartbreaking at best.

"I want a chance to make it right. God knows I'll never have back all her love and devotion, or your trust and respect… but I'll take what I can get."

"Those papers that you have there had better make it crystal clear that those little visits you're hoping for will never take place alone with Suzie."

"I understand the terms," was all Marti said in response to knowing that someone would always be watching her interact with her own child. No matter how old she grew up to be. Marti only hoped that one day Suzie would willingly choose to have her mother in her life. Perhaps the mere hope of that would carry her through her recovery.

Marti's attorney was quick to ask Ben if he had an attorney of his own. Ben did not, but he suggested that he could use the hospital's lawyer. Within thirty minutes, Ben had already made a phone call and Marti's attorney, in turn, emailed his papers to that law office in Cleveland. A prompt read and response came back to them. All that remained was for Ben and Marti to sign their names on a single piece of paper that would officially end their marriage. And then the only thing left to bind them for the next sixteen years was Marti's supervised visitation with their daughter.

Only if Marti could prove to be fit.

# Chapter 24

Jacobi was occupied with a patient when Ben made it back to the OB floor. Reeda immediately wanted to know what happened. "It's not what we thought," Ben spoke with his voice kept low, and then he flipped the switch to business. He had patients waiting.

Two hours went by before either of them crossed paths. All Jacobi had known was what Reeda relayed to her. *It wasn't what we thought.*

Jacobi saw him first. He held a patient's chart in his hand. She met her eyes with his. "Got a minute?" he asked her, and she led him down the hall and into her office. She felt everyone's eyes on them in that office space. Perhaps they should have just called another meeting in the conference room to share their private business all at once.

Ben closed the door and Jacobi just stood there, waiting.

"I know we both expected something bad. She didn't try to harm herself. Just the opposite, actually." Jacobi listened raptly, refraining from interrupting as Ben spoke. "She had an attorney waiting for me. She filed for a divorce with an agenda... I had to agree to supervised visitation between her and Suzie when she gets well."

"I'm still stuck on the fact that Marti took action to divorce you. I really thought that she would fight you forever on that."

"I know it," Ben agreed. "Everything happened so fast. I had the hospital attorney assure me that the papers were legit, and then we both signed."

"That doesn't even seem real," Jacobi sympathized with them right now. As odd as it would seem to anyone else, she also felt this loss.

"That's not all," Ben added, and Jacobi wondered if she had to prepare herself to hear something worse. "She's gone; she's no longer downstairs in the psych ward."

"What? They released her already?" That scared her.

"Not from being in a mental health facility altogether. It seems that Marti requested a transfer to a place in Michigan that's reviewed as one of the top in the country. She wants to increase her chances of getting well. She left today." Ben couldn't assume that he would be notified when they admitted her there, or for any other reason, because he was no longer her husband.

"So just like that? She divorced you and left the state?" Jacobi found all of it difficult to believe.

"Since the day of the car accident, our lives have been caught up in this whirlwind, and oddly Marti seemed to agree."

"Can you truly believe her?" Jacobi had to ask him that.

Ben shrugged. "She's the one who rushed the end of our marriage and left town."

"You make it sound like she just up and left on her own free will. She has a long way to go in another mental health facility. Didn't it bother her to know that she's going to be so far away?"

"I think that's what she wants."

"She probably feels alone regardless." Jacobi wished she could have talked to her first. Not to change her mind, but just to try to understand what she was thinking. Was her long-range plan truly to overcome the mental illness that plagued her and then gradually make her way back into Suzie's life?

"She wanted me to give you this," Ben reached into his pocket for an envelope and then handed it over to Jacobi. "Maybe it will give you some clarity?"

She was afraid to open it, so she just held it in her hand. "What about you, Ben? What do you need?"

"Closure," he responded. "And, today, I feel like Marti gave me a jumpstart on that. I mean, it isn't going to be easy to raise Suzie without her mother, and even when she's ready for those supervised visits —which is all she will ever have— it's going to be awkward and confusing for all of us."

Jacobi imagined the same scenario. She fidgeted with the paper in her hand. "I'm nervous to read her letter."

"You two had a close friendship, so I'm going to stay out of that unless you want to share something with me, okay?"

"That's considerate of you."

Ben smiled. "I'm a considerate kind of guy."

"Can we talk about something later?" she asked him outright.

"Dinner tonight? My house plus Sooz?"

She laughed, as she knew they could talk privately after bedtime.

"Jacobi?" he had that look in his eyes, like he wanted to pull her into his arms and never let her go. And right about now, she needed him to.

But his phone rang with a patient emergency and he had to leave.

Jacobi sat down at her desk. She set the envelope down and stared at it. Leave it to Marti to have the last word, she thought. She just hoped she could handle what she was about to read. Because, the truth was, she too needed some closure right now.

She could hear her own pulse in her ears as she reached for the letter on her desktop and finally opened it.

*Jacobi,*

*By the time you're reading this, I'll be on my way to another destination. My lockup for a while. At least until I reach the point where I can say that I'm okay again. But what exactly is okay when I'm starting completely over with my life utterly alone?*

*I look back on Ben and I... and I realize that I've always had the greater need in our relationship. For what it's worth, I still need him, but that counts for nothing now.*

*I've often wondered if you ever knew that you were my one true friend in my lifetime. Sometimes I believed you understood me better than my own husband. This goes without saying, because I know your heart, but please be everything my daughter needs in a mother. We both know I turned out to be a piss-poor one.*

*I live with a remorse, rooted in my soul now, that will eventually bury me. Meanwhile, I've sworn that I will take the medication, listen to the therapists, and continue to tell myself it's all mind over matter. The truth is, Cobi, I'm done. I have nothing left to give.*

*This place in Michigan will suit me well. It will be a fresh start. Away from the people who look at me and already know my story. Away from being locked up and guarded in the basement of the same hospital where the king and queen reign on the OB floor.*

*I wanted to write a letter to Suzie, for her to open and read when she's much older, but I couldn't find the words. Please tell her one day how sorry I am that I failed her and that I will understand if she cannot forgive me. I was never able to forgive my own mother either.*

*Goodbye, my dearest friend. I do honestly believe that neither one of us ever thought it would end this way.*

*Love,*

*Marti*

## Nothing Left to Give

Jacobi folded the letter, slipped it back into the envelope, and placed it inside the top drawer of her desk. All the while, she had tears spilling out of her eyes and falling down her cheeks. People on the outside, looking at their lives, would be quick to judge them.

*Jacobi, the homewrecker.*

*Marti, a crazed woman, tried to hurt her own child.*

*Ben, the cheater.*

Be it as it may seem — not the way it had truly been.

Jacobi sat at her desk, contemplating if she should intervene once again. Marti needed to be on suicide watch. *Would she be under constant surveillance at this new replacement facility? And for how long? Or would it eventually even matter if Jacobi tried to prolong the inevitable?*

Marti said so herself, she had nothing left to give.

Jacobi came to the realization that it was time to let her be. Suzie was safe. Ben had gotten closure. And now, Jacobi had been on the receiving end of a heartfelt goodbye, in which Marti had reassured her that she was not to blame.

*Goodbye, my dearest friend. I do honestly believe that neither one of us ever thought it would end this way.*

# Chapter 25

A few minutes before five o'clock, Jacobi sent Ben a text.

*Going to be late for dinner. I've got a momma in labor; dilated to a 6. Save me a plate.*

~

Reeda stayed late to assist with the delivery. At one point, when they had some downtime, she approached Jacobi. "I heard the news," she began. "She divorced him and requested an out-of-state transfer, all in a split second."

Jacobi nodded her head. "Does anyone actually work here? Seems to me like there's too much time for gossip."

"Is it true?"

"Yes, Marti gave us all a little closure today."

"Let's hope her troubled soul can find some for herself as well."

"Absolutely," was all Jacobi said in response. She undoubtedly wondered if Marti would lose her battle and give up on herself, but she also realized that any outcome was now out of her hands.

~

There was such a thing as a perfect, uneventful labor, where everything went as expected and the baby's arrival didn't linger for hours on end. Jacobi was grateful to be done, as she was feeling queasy and lightheaded. She needed to eat something before she left for Ben's house. She made a b-line for the locker room where she regularly kept snacks to refuel her body when she worked overtime, and lately that pick-me-up had been crackers. For obvious reasons.

She was just about to pull the door open when someone else pushed it too hard from the other side. The combination of the force and the fact that Jacobi's head already had felt detached from her body, ultimately led her to lose her sense of balance. The last thing she remembered was how she tried to catch herself before she went down, but then her world suddenly went dark.

~

Jacobi thought she heard voices. She attempted to open her eyes, but all her eyelids could do for her was flutter and then close again. Rest. She needed rest. She was so tired. The baby growing inside her, only about the size of a poppyseed, had already taken a toll on her energy level. *The baby!* The thought forced her to open her eyes at once. She had to tell someone that she was pregnant. She needed to be reassured that the baby was okay after the fall.

Both Reeda and Ben were hovering over her. And Suzie could be heard playing in the background, on the chair behind them.

"Hi," Ben spoke, and though his smile was fuzzy to her, she welcomed seeing it. "I hear you went down."

Jacobi nodded. "How embarrassing."

"Oh don't be embarrassed," Reeda nearly scolded her. "All that matters is everything is okay. No broken bones, no concussion. You must have landed mostly on that cute little tushy of yours."

Ben laughed. Jacobi was still worried about everything being okay. Namely, her unborn baby.

"I'll leave you two to talk," Reeda offered to take Suzie for a treat from the vending machine, and Ben agreed. Jacobi waved at Suzie as they left the room.

"So much for our dinner plans," Ben teased her.

"Did Reeda call you? She should have waited until she knew that I was fine."

"No way. I wanted to be here the moment I heard. Suzie did, too."

Jacobi smiled. "Thank you."

"It's part of my responsibility," he noted.

"I'm a big girl. Been taking care of myself for a long time."

He nodded in agreement. "Right. You sure have. Things change, though. And sometimes making room in our hearts for additions in our lives is just what the doctor ordered."

"What are you talking about?" her confusion forced her not to read too much into his words.

"After you fell, Reeda rushed to your side… and that's when you told her to make sure the baby was alright. At first she thought you were referring to the one you had just delivered, but she quickly caught on that you're pregnant." There was a light in Ben's eyes that Jacobi had not seen in, what felt like, a very long time. "We're having a baby!" His smile was wide.

"Such a nice way for you to find out. I was going to tell you, I promise, I was."

"When? Six months from now when you're waddling down the hallway?"

"Stop being an ass," she laughed a little. "Please. Seriously. The baby is fine, right?"

"Yes, our baby is just fine."

"Our baby," Jacobi repeated.

She harbored dreams that she believed would end up being unfulfilled in her lifetime, simply because some things were not meant to be. Then, when everything shifted, their lives together were significantly altered. And now, it was true what they said about a baby symbolizing a new beginning.

# Epilogue

Eleven years later...

On the third story of their townhouse, Jacobi entered one side of the Jack and Jill bedroom that was shared between 13-year-old Suzie and 10-year-old Grey. With a full-size bathroom in between, the siblings occupied that shared space combined with their own privacy. They were closely bonded, however, and most times they spent their time being together up there.

Suzie gave Jacobi an unwelcomed look when she entered her room without knocking. "In my defense, my hands are full," Jacobi noted as she piled three hoodies and two t-shirts on top the duvet, where Suzie lounged and was distracted with the smart phone in her hands.

A moment later, Suzie set the phone down and called Jacobi's attention away from the laundry. "Cobi?" She still sentimentally called her that after all these years. It just stuck as suitable, and Jacobi thought it was perfect. Through the years she had not wanted her stepdaughter to fall into a pattern of calling her mommy, or mom. It wasn't an appropriate way to honor the place that Marti once had in her daughter's life. "Can I ask you something?"

"Anything," Jacobi assured her. The two of them were closely bonded. Suzie had not been a dramatic pre-teen, and now as a teenager she was mature and responsible, which couldn't have made her dad and Jacobi prouder. Their lives were hectic, having both parents as doctors in a shared private practice of their own now, which was thriving after nearly eight years. Cleveland Clinic had given them a wonderful start to their careers, but they had since moved on from there, together.

"I'm older now, and I want to know some things." Again, Jacobi heard the voice of a 13-year-old who was wise beyond her years. She did momentarily wonder if she should sit down for this. Instead, she thought it would be better to be ready to pace. "Why didn't my mom ever come back?" There were photographs of Marti in their home. She was never someone that Ben nor Jacobi ever wanted Suzie to forget. Suzie, being only a toddler then, needed those visual reminders and for her dad and Jacobi to talk about Marti. "I know you've said that she was sick and tried to get better."

Jacobi sat down on the bed, beside the laundry. "When your mom was about your age, her father left her mother." It was strange for Suzie to process that the people she was hearing about were her grandparents, yet she had never met them, she hadn't even known their names. "That woman, who would be your grandmother now, reeled from the loss of her marriage, and she took her own life."

"Oh that's bad. I mean, I could not imagine right now in my life not having you, Cobi. You're my mom."

Jacobi's heart swelled to hear those words. "Oh, sweetie, you sure know how to get to me, right here," she placed her hand over her own chest. She regrouped her thoughts for a moment and then began to choose her words carefully. It was time for Suzie to know what happened to Marti. Jacobi wondered if this truth should have come directly from Ben, but he was not the one who Suzie reached out to just now.

"I think deep down your mom never dealt with the loss of her own mother," or so that seemed to make sense to Jacobi through the years. "Marti was a woman who knew what she wanted and she always got it. She just had a way of being in control. Your dad and I met before he met your mom. The best way to say this is that he and I always had real feelings for each other, but we focused on med school and our friendship instead of getting involved. Then, he met your mother. Your dad loved her, don't think otherwise. They were married for five years, and their love created you. But sometimes, I guess, just like the relationship with your grandparents all those years ago, things change, people fall out of love."

"So it was my dad who fell out of love with my mom, because he chose you?" Suzie's question was direct and a little difficult to hear as she began to connect the dots.

"Your mom and dad lost two babies after they had you," Jacobi tried to fill in the blanks to explain why there was pain and perhaps a cause for them to grow apart in their marriage. "Your mom, again I think just like when she lost her own mother, kept some tough feelings inside. She wanted another baby so badly." Jacobi paused. "Then, the final burden for her was when your dad wanted to leave."

"Did he leave her for you? Did you love him then?"

"I've always loved him. That's the thing about our relationship… we should have just grabbed ahold of how we felt about each other from the very beginning. Marti would never have gotten hurt that way. But, that's not how it happened… because we know that we were supposed to have you in our lives. You, and your brother, are our greatest blessings."

"Cobi? Do you think my mom ever wanted to come back… to at least see me again?"

"Your mom put you in harm's way when you were little," Jacobi was incredibly cautious with how she explained this story. "She didn't want to live anymore, if she could not have your dad. She also had a very difficult time with knowing that your dad would likely move on with his life, with you, and with me… and maybe even have another child. That image haunted her, and it ultimately drove her to do things that she never would have done otherwise. Marti was not a bad person, honey. She was just very troubled."

"You defend her when you talk about her. Why?"

"She was my friend. We were close for many years."

"How did she die?"

"She didn't."

Six months after Marti was transferred to the mental health facility in Michigan, she was released. Medication and psychiatric help successfully paved a way for her to regain control of her life. Or, at least that's what she had wanted everyone to believe. She told the doctors and the therapists exactly what they needed to hear. They believed, or at least they had no other choice but to trust, that Marti was mentally balanced and able to survive in a world opposite of being surrounded by people who watched and evaluated her every move.

Jacobi still had the letter from Marti. It was a blatant reminder of how quickly life could change. She kept it to one day be able to relay Marti's message to Suzie.

"We've never heard from your mother again. I have a letter from her that she wrote to me before she left Cleveland. In it, she didn't dwell too much on faulting me or your dad. She basically honored our friendship with a somewhat peaceful goodbye. She was still tormented then, but she asked me to be everything that you needed in a mother. And she wanted me to tell you, one day, how sorry she was for failing you. She wrote about how she would understand if you could not forgive her, as she was never able to forgive her own mother either."

Suzie was quiet, as if she was taking all of this in and trying to process what did or did not happen with her mother. *If she had gotten better, why didn't she ever reach out to her child? If she was still struggling with her life, what had prevented her from giving up altogether like her own mother had done?*

"I wish there was more for me to tell you. Your dad and I have also lived with some of those lingering, unanswered questions." Jacobi hoped the truth, all that she had known about Marti, was enough to help Suzie at this point in her life. Yes, she was old enough to understand, but acceptance was difficult at any age.

"I wonder if she ever was able to have more children," Suzie shared her immediate thoughts with Jacobi.

"That thought has also crossed my mind," Jacobi admitted. "You know, there are ways to find out if you have a DNA match out there, if one day you're interested in tracking down a potential sibling."

Suzie shrugged. "That's not on my radar at all. I just wanted to know about my mom. Honestly, Grey is enough for me."

Jacobi was smiling with tears in her eyes. "I think this might be a good time for me to remind you that you are a remarkable young girl. I want you to always believe in yourself and never allow anyone or anything that comes your way in life to make you feel like you are not enough, or as if you have nothing left to give this world."

"Why did you tell me that? I mean, I know my worth, Cobi."

She was so proud of this child. Just bursting at the seams with pride and joy for who she was becoming. "I have every confidence in you," Jacobi reached for her hand from across the bed. "I just wish—"

"Your wish," Suzie interrupted her, "I'll bet is the same as mine. I wish that my mom would have had someone like you in her life when she was my age, someone to tell her that she was special and to make her feel loved. I think that would have been enough to save her from herself."

# About the Author

There are all types of people that we meet along the way in our lives, and some will stay and always remain right there for us in some capacity. For Jacobi and Ben, their lives were intertwined on multiple levels and every aspect kept pulling them back to each other. We root for people like that to find each other. We all hope to experience a connection like that in our own lives.

A character like Marti symbolizes how many people are suffering and barely holding themselves together. They live their lives suppressing pain or trauma. In turn, they don't see what's good or what's harmful, or what they should or should not be doing to save themselves. In the end, I do think that Marti held herself accountable for her own actions.

Perhaps the message that I was going for when writing this story was that there are ways to get through hardship, to not let it drown us but to allow it to make us stronger, better human beings.

As always, thank you for reading!

love,

Lori Bell

Made in the USA
Columbia, SC
17 March 2022